Star Bright!

A CHRISTMAS STORY

Andrew M. Greeley

Star Bright!

A CHRISTMAS STORY

A TOM DOHERTY ASSOCIATES BOOK
NEW YORK

This is a work of fiction. All the characters and events portrayed in this book are either products of the author's imagination or are used fictitiously.

STARBRIGHT!

A Forge Book
Published by Tom Doherty Associates, LLC
175 Fifth Avenue
New York, NY 10010

www.tor.com

Forge® is a registered trademark of Tom Doherty Associates, LLC.

ISBN 0-765-34981-7
EAN 978-0765-34981-1

First edition: September 1997
First mass market edition: November 2004

Printed in the United States of America

0 9 8 7 6 5 4 3 2 1

For my friend John Shea whose book *Star Light* gave me the idea for this story of an angel and Christmas:

> The cave of Christmas
> is hidden
> in the center of the earth.
> You will need a lamp for the journey.
> A man named John
> is a step ahead of you.
> His torch sweeps the ground
> so that you do not stumble.
> He brings you
> at your own pace
> to the entrance of the cave.
> His smile is complete,
> perfect,
> whole,
> lacking nothing.
>
> Inside
> there is a sudden light,
> but it does not hurt your eyes.
> The darkness has been pushed back by radiance.
> You feel like an underwater swimmer
> who has just broken the surface of the Jordan
> and is breathing in the sky.
> John is gone.
> Notice
> from whom the light is shining,
> beloved child.

I am grateful to Professor Walter Connor of the Harvard Russian Research Center for his helpful comments on this story and his masterful correction of my clumsy Russian spelling.

PRELUDE

*"It was said by the very old peasants in my country—
and now it is said again—that on some very special Christmas nights Mary and Joseph and the
Child come back to earth. There is snow on the
ground and the nights are cold but not too cold.
The blanket of stars in the sky is like a blanket of
spring flowers. The angels and the shepherds and
the shepherds' children and the twelve wise men
come with them."*

"Twelve?" I asked. "I thought there were only
three."

"We Russians know better," Odessa said waving
my question aside as a silly interruption. "It is also
said that when men and women of faith who know

where the cave is enter it to gaze on the child, they see something truly amazing."

"What's that?"

"They see that the face of the Child is their own face. Then they realize they are the beloved child! Is that not wondrous!"

It sounded like pantheism to me, but what did I know? I was nothing more than an Irish kid from the South Side of Chicago. How did I get mixed up with a Russian mystic who made Alyosha Karamazov look like an earthbound nerd?

"My family," I observed, "engages in gladiatorial mayhem on Christmas. I'm the referee who is supposed to make peace."

"What a shame," Odessa shook her head in sadness. "They will not see the beloved Child. As the Russian proverb says, he who fears wolves will never go into the woods."

I didn't see how the proverb fit, but I had enough sense not to ask.

I had made a mistake when I invited her to come home with me for Christmas. Our date for the festival was not the same as the Russian date. Christmas was not the great feast in the East that it had become in the West. We were not seriously involved with one another, at least I didn't think we were. My solemn, mystical grand duchess would not fit with the South Side Irish, especially my contentious manic family.

In a burst of sentimentality I had felt sorry for her that she would be alone on Christmas Day, a thoroughly American and totally absurd compassion. If Odessa wanted to be with others on that day, she didn't need my help. Moreover she was used to being alone. In fact, she loved being alone.

The sadness in her vast brown eyes had been too much for me. Sad-eyed women are always too much for me. Odessa's eyes were always sad; that goes with being Russian.

So now I was going to pour water on the oil.

Or perhaps to be more precise, vodka.

We Flanigans are good Irish Catholics. We believe in God, but we rarely mention him save when we take His name in vain in exclamations of anger or surprise or merely emphasis. Odessa, however, talks about God all the time, as though He were someone present in the room with us. You can't have that kind of talk in an Irish Catholic family that lives in an Irish Catholic neighborhood like ours, can you?

CHAPTER

1

"Good morning, miss," I said in Russian. *"I hope the* news you are reading is good news."

I had noticed the young woman reading a Russian paper on a bench at the edge of Harvard Square. I wanted to show off my skill in the Russian language. I had no idea whether she was attractive or not—the audience does not have to be beautiful for me to want to perform.

I certainly wasn't trying to pick her up.

Come on, Flanigan, would you have used the same line if she were not a young woman?

Maybe.

She recoiled in shock, covering herself with her paper as though I had discovered her naked.

"Who are you?" she demanded in Russian, momentarily terrified.

Oh, boy, another mistake.

I turned on my best smile.

"My name is Jack Flanigan and I'm a harmless American of Irish origins. I was just showing off my Russian."

I am not, to be candid about it, a very prepossessing guy. I'm five ten if I stretch and am skinny. I could hardly be any sort of athlete, not in most sports anyway. My freckled face is kind of pinched and my wire-brush red hair often looks like I'm sort of a Dennis Rodman freak. So I get by on my smile.

The young woman considered me very carefully, as well she might.

I had wandered across the Yard after my class and towards the Square where I would catch the MBTA for my return ride to Chestnut Hill and Boston College. It was a lovely late October day, a delayed Indian summer with a touch of color still in the trees. I had been indulging myself in feelings of superiority over the Harvard weirdos who were creeping and crawling around, most of them apparently engaged in profound thought, if one were to judge by the pained expressions on their faces. I suppose that if by some astonishing mistake they had come out to Chestnut Hill they would have thought the denizens there were weirdos too.

But they were, you see, my kind of weirdos.

Her face was spectacularly exotic—pale skin framed by long, straight, and carefully brushed black hair. It was not, however, your classic oval Slavic face. Rather her broad forehead, high cheekbones, and triangular facial lines together with an ever so slight a slant in her eyes suggested the steppes—those endless rolling plains between the Volga and the Urals across which Asian armies had swept for a couple of millennia. Her large, liquid brown eyes hinted at the pain and the glory of all those millennia. Her face was innocent of expression as she pondered what sort of freak I might be.

"Your accent is excellent," she said softly in English, her voice a low alto. "You have lived in my country?"

I didn't even intend my comment to be a good opening line, not really. Or at least not mostly.

"Last three summers," I said in Russian.

"You have a Moscow accent."

"I spent time there. St. Petersburg. Volgograd,

Irkutsk, Vladivostok. All kinds of places."

She inclined her head slightly. Maybe that meant approval, or at least not disapproval.

"You rode the Trans-Siberian?"

"Had to."

She nodded again.

Maybe all that meant was understanding.

She folded up her paper and rested it on the thighs of her faded jeans—standard issue for women students of her age.

"What did you think of my country?"

Mind you, her face remained utterly immobile.

"I loved the Russian people. Delightful folk. They deserve better."

Again she inclined her head, a little deeper this time as if to indicate that my answer was acceptable.

"Could I buy you a cup of coffee and a doughnut to make up for scaring you?" I asked in English.

"Why would you want to do that?" she replied in English which was arguably better than mine—no Chicago "a" in it.

"Practice my Russian."

She smiled, which is to say that the corners of

her lips moved up slightly and a few perfect teeth appeared briefly.

"You are trying to pick me up?"

"Not really. I mean not really, but kind of maybe. I was only showing off."

Another nod and another faint smile.

"Tea of course, not coffee," she said standing up and slinging the inevitable book bag over her wide and supple shoulders. "And a doughnut."

"Tea certainly," I replied, taking her arm to guide her through the traffic in the Square.

I then realized that the young woman was a grand duchess. She belonged not in Harvard Square wearing running shoes and a white sweatshirt with the name of the school emblazoned in dull crimson. Rather she should be dancing to waltz music in a vast ballroom in St. Petersburg, or more likely Moscow. She should be dressed in an elaborate gown (bare shoulders) and surrounded by gorgeous women and handsome men in colorful uniforms.

She was tall (taller than I am) and willowy and achingly graceful in her gestures and movements, with a narrow waist, long legs, and rich and glorious breasts. She walked across the street serenely, as though the whole of Harvard and all its environs were hers, and complacently, as though she knew that everyone was looking at her and didn't care. There were no aristocrats left in Russia. The children of the ruling class were without class. Somehow a few aristocratic genes must have survived and shaped this goddesslike grand duchess.

I exaggerate? No way.

It is generally known that when young men encounter an attractive woman, their imaginations hastily undress her. I am no different from other young men, though I was both respectful and cautious—the latter because of traffic in the Square and the former because you gotta be respectful to your grand duchesses.

(A priest once told me that older men do the same thing and that, if men didn't do that, the species would have long since died out. The advantage older men enjoy, he added, is that their taste in what is attractive is much broader than that of someone your age, so there are many more women about whom to fantasize. Only a priest would dare say something like that.)

"Your name is John," she said in English when

we completed our dangerous pilgrimage across the street. "Therefore I will call you Ivan when we speak Russian."

"All right," I replied in Russian as I guided her, my hand on the small of her back as though I were leading her to the dance floor, toward the door of one of the better coffee shops. "What shall I call you?"

"You may call me Odessa."

No Russian young woman was called Odessa. But, under the circumstances, so what?

"I was there," I replied as I held the door open for her. "Steps down to the sea, Eisenstein, Potemkin, that kind of thing. Cosmopolitan place. Belongs to Ukraine now."

"Odessa will never belong to anyone."

"The city or the woman?"

She turned her head to look at me as I held the chair for her.

"Both."

She removed a large notebook from her bag and began to write. She tilted it on the table so I could not see what she was writing.

I ordered a pot of tea and four doughnuts. She continued to scribble or perhaps to draw.

"You're a student across the way?" I asked her.

She tilted her head forward, more interested in her work than in conversation.

"Senior. Art history."

"You go on for a doctorate?"

"Perhaps."

"You will return to Russia?"

"Perhaps."

"I'm at B.C. They let me in here to take a course every week."

"B.C.?"

She did not look up.

"Uh, Boston College. Jesuit institution over in Chestnut Hill."

"Ah."

The teapot, three tea bags on the saucer, and the plate of doughnuts arrived.

She sighed and closed her notebook.

"I admire you Americans very much. You are a wonderful people with a marvelous culture. But you have no sense of the importance of ceremony. Unless one does important things like making tea properly, one does not thank God adequately for the gift. Is that not so?"

I was enchanted by the mystery and the magic in her wondrous brown eyes.

"If you say so."

"God did not have to give us tea, did he, Ivan?"

"I guess not."

Eyes fixed on her work, she opened the tea bags, lifted the top off the pot of water, and stirred the leaves into the water with elaborate solemnity, almost as though tea making were a sacrament. Apparently it was for her.

Then she collected my tea cup and placed it next to hers. She opened the cover of the pot to stir the brewing tea once. With another sigh, she spread a doubled paper napkin over each cup and poured out the tea with a movement not unlike a priest pouring wine into a chalice. She offered me my cup with a bow. Finally she extended the platter of doughnuts in my direction with yet another bow.

Holy Communion.

If she were a grand duchess I was at least a prince. Ivan. Prince Ivan the what? Ivan the Idiot perhaps.

"Thank you, Odessa," I said gravely.

"Now we honor God when we drink our tea and eat our doughnut," she said with equal gravity.

What's with this God stuff, I wondered, glancing around to make sure that the deity had not slipped into the coffee shop.

Russians are a people with an opulent and often exuberant love of ceremony, drunk or sober. Even the backbreaking poverty in which most of them still live had not stamped it out completely. There is always a touch of ceremony in the serving of tea. But the little ritual in which I was participating was unusual.

We exchanged biographical information as young people do on their first encounter. My father was a surgeon, my mother a lawyer. I was from Chicago. I had three siblings, an older brother and sister, and a teenage sister. I was majoring in Russian studies because Russia had fascinated me after I had seen the revolution of 1991 live on CNN. I was probably going to law school back in Chicago next year but I would always be interested in Russia. I had applied to Harvard but, despite my ninety-ninth percentile score and my merit scholarship, I had been turned down because the university's view of multiculturalism did not have room for a Jesuit-trained Irish Catholic from Chicago.

The last was unnecessary but I was still angry.

She tilted her head forward in what might be sympathy, refilled my tea cup, and offered me a second doughnut.

Her bio was much more jejune. She was an only child. Her father had been a colonel in the Red Army and had died in Afghanistan. Her mother also had been a surgeon. She too was dead. They were both with God and happy together. She was at Harvard because some very important people in Russia whose son's life her father had saved insisted that she accept a scholarship in his memory, a scholarship which would also pay for her graduate studies later on. She worked as a translator at the Russian Research Center. She belonged to Winthrop House where she still ate most of her meals. They had given her permission to live in her own apartment after her first year because it was easier to adjust to American culture and language. She had thought about returning there for her senior year, but it would have been too much work to move.

"Do you go to divine worship?" she asked me, returning to her tablet.

"Sure, usually anyway."

"At your school?"

"The Jesuits have masses going on all day long."

"Sometimes I go to St. Paul and sometimes to St. Vladimir. The separation between the two churches is absurd. I like divine worship at St.

Paul. It is solemn and rich but never too stuffy. Sometimes at St. Vladimir it is too stuffy. And," slight upturn of her lips, "too long."

That was a long speech for my elegant and lovely grand duchess.

"Your family was religious?"

"Of course. Both my grandfathers were priests. Secretly."

"So you've always been a believer?"

"Oh, no. I was a candidate member of the young communists. Religion was the opiate. I was rebelling, I suppose. Then at Easter in 1989, the first real Easter many of us ever knew, I was filled with God's grace and love."

She lifted her right shoulder in a gesture which would become familiar. It meant something like the New York phrase, "what can I tell you?"

It also temporarily disturbed the alignment of her breasts, an effect which produced pure delight in my hungry fantasy.

"My life has been very different since then. I am very happy now. Usually."

Enough God talk for now.

She opened her notebook and began scrawling again. No, she was drawing something.

"Young woman, are you drawing a picture of me?"

"Sketching you," she corrected me.

"You're an artist?"

She shrugged her shoulder again.

"Perhaps."

She continued to scribble, now with considerable vigor.

"We all share in God's work of creation, of course; artists, however, more than others. They help us to see what is really there, what God intends to say, the revelation of grace in a person or a place or an event."

"I see."

I really didn't see at all. However, religion on the lips of my grand duchess seemed attractive, vital, even exciting.

"Can I see what you're doing?"

"No," she said firmly. "Not yet."

"I guess I should be flattered that you're sketching me."

She looked up from her tablet, pondered me, and then dismissed what I had said with a wave of her hand, another gesture with which I would become familiar.

"I sketch many different things."

I had finished my second doughnut. She had left hers alone. Our tête-à-tête was drawing to a close. Did I want to see her again? Yeah, I did. All right, how did I find an opening to say that?

"There," she said, turning her sketch book toward me. "It is not finished, but it will show you what I see."

The kid in the sketch was a nice boy, possibly even attractive, with a great smile and terribly vulnerable eyes. I didn't like that last bit. Jack Flanigan is not vulnerable, repeat, he is *not* vulnerable.

"It's wonderful," I said, trying the smile again. "It's far too good looking to be me."

"Your mother would say, Ivan, that it is a perfect insight into you."

What did my mother have to do with it?

"Only a face a mother can love?"

"Of course not."

"Can I send it to my mother?"

"When I am finished. . . . Now I must go to class. . . . May I take this doughnut with me?"

"Sure. . . . When are you going to finish the sketch?"

"Perhaps next Tuesday," she said, putting the sketch pad away.

"Next Tuesday?"

She stood up and slung the book bag over her shoulder.

"Did you not say you have class here on Tuesday and Thursday mornings?"

"Uh, yeah."

"You do not wish to practice your Russian any more, Ivan? . . . Perhaps not. It is very good. Besides, as the proverb says, he who likes to ski downhill had better enjoy climbing uphill."

What on earth did that mean?

"Certainly I want to keep practicing my Russian."

"Then I will see you at the bench across the street on Tuesday. Thank you for the tea and the doughnut."

That settled that.

Or did it? She had drawn a flattering and dangerously discerning sketch of me. She wanted to see me again. Did this stunning, mystic grand duchess actually *like* me? Why?

It was a disturbing prospect. Maybe I should run. Maybe I should not show up four days hence. I knew, however, that I would. Captured already? Or enchanted? Maybe she was a witch as well as a mystic. In Russia such things could happen.

As I rode back to B.C. on the red and the green lines, I lost myself in fantasy. She was the Grand Duchess Odessa. I was Prince Ivan the Brave— hell, I said it was fantasy. At first she could not admit that she loved me because she was destined to marry an elderly general in the Tsar's army. But he was killed at Smolensk. At the end of the fantasy, I carried her in her night dress from her palace as Moscow burned and Napoleon's army entered the city.

I arrived at Chestnut Hill before I could finish the fantasy.

Odessa was there the next Tuesday, another glorious Indian summer day, and with her were three little girls, a little boy, and two smiling mothers. She was telling the kids a story. She nodded towards the place next to her on the bench and went on with the story.

It was an elaborate tale featuring a beautiful princess named Vasilisa the Wise, a helpful witch named Baba Yaga, and a young prince, handsome but not too bright, named Ivan the Red. I had the impression, which later would be confirmed often, that Odessa made up the stories as she went along. The kids were bug-eyed and the mothers seemed enthralled too. At the ending Vasilisa the Wise and Baba Yaga rescued the prince from a swamp and they all lived happily ever after, "until my next story."

The kids applauded.

"Tell Tatiana 'thank you,' " one of the mothers said.

"Thank you, Tatiana," they said in chorus.

"Tatiana?" I said as they left.

"Another one of my names." A dismissive wave of her hand.

"Vasilisa would be yet another?"

"Vasilisa the Wise," she corrected me.

"What should I call you?" I said in Russian.

"Whatever you wish."

"I like Odessa."

"Do you really?" she said, seemingly surprised. "Shall we go to the coffee shop? This time I have brought Russian tea and a strainer. They would be offended if I brought a samovar I am afraid."

She stood up, slung the inevitable bag over her shoulder, and walked towards the stoplight. Naturally I took her arm. Someone has to protect your grand duchesses when they cross the street.

She had put some care into her physical appearance. She was wearing a Harvard sweater (crimson), tightly fitting black jeans, polished black boots, a blue blouse, and a silver Greek cross around her neck. Her hair was tied in a ponytail and a touch of makeup emphasized the smoothness of her buttermilk complexion.

All this for poor, dumb Ivan the Red?

"I thought we might have a bit of lunch, something a little bit better than a doughnut."

"That is not necessary."

"I didn't say it was. But when Vasilisa the Wise puts on a touch of lipstick, poor dumb, stupid Ivan the Red shouldn't take her to any old coffee shop."

Her face turned the color of her sweater and a noise, kind of like a melodious hum, escaped her lips. I figured that it was the way grand duchesses laugh.

"You are very perceptive, Prince Ivan."

She accepted my ministrations, her arm in mine, then my hand on the small of her back, as I conducted her to a table at the back of an elegant little French restaurant behind the Coop—as we call the Harvard Cooperative Society, where textbooks and just about everything else can be bought.

"This is very nice, Ivan. I have never been here before."

"I'm glad you like it."

We ordered, I my steak, she her fish. We also asked for a pot of boiling water. Somehow Odessa charmed the waitress, obviously a graduate student, with a brief account of how we Russians made tea.

The waitress looked at me skeptically. I might be babbling in Russian, but no way was I anything but Irish, arguably shanty Irish.

As we waited for our food, Odessa removed her sweater, causing my hormones to run wild, and took her sketch pad out of her book bag. I noted that one more button was open on her blouse than absolutely needed to be open.

"I have almost finished it," she informed me. "I must make a few changes, I think."

"You've worked on it since Thursday?"

"Of course."

One eye on me and one eye on the sketch pad, she worked rapidly.

"You may continue to talk, Prince Ivan the Red. It will not distract me."

"God forbid that I interfere with one of His sacrament makers."

That comment did not disturb her in the least.

"God reveals Herself to us through all the people

we encounter in our lives, some of course more than others. We must learn to see God in them, so we value them for what they are, of course, and for what God wants them to be."

That was scary too.

"There, it is finished," she said with a sigh of relief just as our lunches arrived. "I am afraid to show it to you. You do not like to appear as good and as vulnerable as you really are."

She put the sketchbook aside.

Yikes.

"Ivan the Good?"

"Sometimes."

Was this woman trying to seduce me?

Run, Jack Flanigan. You are no Ivan the Good, no way.

She then set about making our tea, the ceremonial taking on greater majesty now that she was working with some of her own tools.

We talked as we ate, mostly about Russian history and politics and the excitement of the "social transformation," as they called the change after the end of socialism.

"We will become a great country again," she said firmly, "a great free, peaceful democracy. Yet so many people suffer."

I agreed.

Then over our ice cream—Russians are if anything crazier about ice cream than Americans—I said, "I'd like to see the sketch."

She picked the book off the empty chair where she had put it, opened it, and turned it towards me. I don't know how a woman with an utterly impassive face can look vulnerable, but somehow she managed it—anxiety in her eyes, I suppose.

I gulped.

She had me perfectly—the wit, the confusions, the self-pity, the anger, and, worst of all, the tenderness about which I was not at all sure. Worse still, she made the sum total look more attractive than I could possibly be.

Tears formed in my eyes. Yeah, I'm a real Irish sentimentalist.

"It's wonderful, Baba Yaga," I said. "You see right through me."

"You think I'm a witch?"

"Or a reader of hearts."

Again the soft humming sound.

"You are quite transparent, Prince Ivan the Good. You should not be troubled by that. . . . You will send it to your mother?"

"Certainly."

No rush to do so. Mom was a smart, shrewd lawyer. She'd sense that the artist was looking at me with what might be the eyes of love.

I did not want to be loved in such a way that there was no place left to hide. Not now. Not ever.

"Are you crying, Prince Ivan?"

"Yep."

"I did not mean to make you cry."

"We Irish cry a lot over silly things. . . . Sorry, this portrait is not silly."

"We Russians cry a lot too."

So there were two of us, seniors at Harvard University, one validly, the other by way of exception, weeping like children.

We'd better get out of here quickly.

We did.

She led me into the Coop, bought two cardboard sheets and a mailing bag, put the sketch between two other pages and the cardboard sheets, placed them in the mailing bag, and gave the bag to me.

It was another ceremony, like a priest breaking the hosts before Communion.

"You *will* send it to your mother?"

"Certainly."

Which in this case meant probably not.

"I have embarrassed you, Ivan."

"I feel like you have taken off all my emotional clothes, Odessa."

"Is that a bad feeling?"

"No," I said honestly enough. "It's kind of good. And it's very new."

"Then you will come to my house for lunch on Thursday. I will make tea properly, with a samovar and Russian china and Russian cake."

How could I refuse?

She gave me a three-by-five card with her address on Summer Road printed neatly in Cyrillic script. Nice touch.

I did a little research the next day in the music section of the B.C. library. I found what I was looking for. I also found a videotape I thought I had remembered.

Why all the bother?

I don't know. Maybe I just wanted to show off that I could sing as well as speak Russian. I'm maybe one step, just possibly two, above the Irish whisky tenors that bore the hell out of you at wedding receptions. No way will I ever be one of those. I hate to admit it publicly, but I even see a voice teacher once a week at B.C. I like to sing and I'd like to be able to do it reasonably well.

The teacher tells me that I have perfect pitch, which will never help me in the courtroom.

I wasn't sure what Odessa/Tatiana had in store for me. She seemed far too religious and far too virtuous to be planning a seduction. Yet there was a strong strain of sexual licentiousness in some kinds of Russian mysticism.

Would I let myself be seduced?

I most fervently hoped not, but then I'd never been a target before, much less a target of such a delicious woman.

I brought along a box of my diminishing supply of raspberry Frango mints from Marshall Field's, which are so delicious as to be venially sinful.

I was less than a happy camper on the ride into Cambridge and through my class on Thursday morning. A cold rain had drifted in from the Atlantic. I hated the end of Indian summer with an irrational passion. Moreover my sister Brigid had phoned me last night in a rage at my parents. Brigie, a redhead like me, though on her it looks good, is a tall, lovely young woman with good taste and common sense on all subjects save her mother and father. They didn't know how to deal with her, never having had anyone quite like her around the house. They tried to impose rules on her that had never applied to the three older children. She thought they were hypocrites when they pretended to virtue and yet fought with each other. She hated my father, she told me, because he was a rude, crude, stupid man. She hated my mother because she put up with my father. They ought to get a divorce, Brigie insisted. Indeed, Brigie contended, my mother actually had talked about divorce.

I didn't believe that, not quite.

My father is a hardhead, a jerk, a loudmouth—and one of the best surgeons in the city. Not all surgeons are like him, I hasten to add, though a lot of them are. My mother is a tough trial lawyer who does not suffer fools gladly, and my father was becoming more of a fool with each passing year, though he was still in his early fifties. Usually she just tuned him out, but either he was becoming more obnoxious or her patience was wearing thin. I'd been the peacemaker all my life and hated the role, which is why I went away to school and spent my summers in Russia. Brigie was not the mediator type: She combined the virtues and defects of both of them.

The goofy thing about the conflicts is that my father is not a jerk at heart. He is generous, compassionate with his patients, loyal to his friends, does not drink, much less engage in violence with my mother, and means well. He had spent two months, at some risk to his life, in Bosnia doing emergency surgery, probably treating his Bosnian patients with the same apparent arrogance that he directs at his American patients. Dad is a firm believer in equal opportunity arrogance. Yet he had supported me vigorously when I was accused of cheating in the golf tournament last summer, though he thought my trips to Russia were proof that I had become a Communist.

He was behind the door, alas, when sensitivity was passed out—and the ability to keep his big, loud Irish mouth shut.

I doubted that there was any love left between the two of them. Maybe divorce would not be a bad idea. My mother, a handsome, lively woman, perhaps could find someone better. Dad would never find anyone as patient.

But what does a son know about the passion that may still bind his parents together?

So I was not in a good mood as I walked against the wind and the rain after my class. I managed to get lost and finally arrived fifteen minutes late at the wooden house with outside stairs on that edge of the Cambridge slum that was changing over to Harvard fringe.

I slipped a couple of times on the rickety stairs as I climbed to the tiny third-floor garret.

"Ivan," she said nervously as she opened the door after my first knock, "I was worried about you."

"I got lost," I said sheepishly.

Odessa/Tatiana was dressed as though my visit was a state occasion—a tailored beige suit with matching sweater, nylons, high heels, a ring, a pendant, and earrings. Her hair was piled on top of her head. Her mid-thigh miniskirt enabled me to confirm my suspicion that her legs were beautiful too—long and slender and strong. She was a grand duchess whose accumulated height was now several inches above mine.

She thanked me for the box of Frango mints.

My fantasies about seduction were soon erased. I discovered that there were not one but two priests in her tiny apartment—and one priest's wife.

"This is Ivan," she said to the crowd.

The older priest was the thin, enthusiastic, and brilliant pastor of St. Paul's who had lectured last year at B.C.

"Jack Flanigan, Father." I shook his hand.

"Tim O'Brien," he replied.

I spoke in Russian to Peter, the priest from St. Vladimir's, and his wife Annah. Their replies were hesitant. They were Americans, and my Russian was better than theirs. His face was round and Slavic and his blond beard was neatly trimmed. His wife was short and pretty and obviously worshipped him.

"Now one glass vodka," the grand duchess announced. "Then I make tea and we eat."

They'd been waiting for me. She had been afraid I might have changed my mind.

She removed a bottle of vodka from a tiny refrigerator. In Russia you don't weaken it with ice, you serve it cold. One glass in the Russian worldview meant one full glass, enough to wipe me out for the rest of the afternoon.

"We should thank God for this wonderful gift which helps us to relax and celebrate," she said, "and is a great gift so long as we have only one glass. We pray for those who must drink more than one glass."

You bet, Tatiana. One quarter of the men in Russia are chronic alcoholics. Male life expectancy is declining. Russian vodka bottles come with flip top caps like our soda cans because it is unimaginable that a bottle, once opened, will not be finished immediately.

I looked around the apartment—a small parlor, an even smaller bedroom, a closetlike kitchenette. It was flawlessly neat and clean: books and articles in orderly stacks, a tiny desk empty save for a very old Apple computer, walls covered with her carefully arranged drawings. Most of the sketches were in chalk or pencil or crayon. An oil painting of a beautiful woman, her mother no doubt, wearing the same jewelry. Also a crayon sketch of a shy and modest nude. Self-portrait, perhaps. I told myself to keep my eyes off it during lunch; or at least not get caught gawking at it.

On the other hand she knew I was coming. If she objected to my admiration of her charms, she should have put it away somewhere. Shouldn't she?

We stood in a solemn circle. Some big deal. I looked at the cake next to the old samovar. Birthday cake. Flanigan, you jerk. Well, at least I'd brought her some candy. No way I was going to sing my song in front of a crowd. That'd be a performance, and I hadn't come to perform. Some other time.

"We are here," Father Peter began, "to celebrate Tatiana Alekseevna's twenty-first birthday. She now can legally buy vodka in this country."

Slight titter. It was, I gathered, the birthday queen's turn to talk.

"I am very grateful to you, my friends, for coming to this small birthday party. I am grateful to God for giving me the great gift of life and for lending me for a time my parents who taught me so much about God. I miss them but I am happy that they are with God and are joining in this celebration. I have been given so much and have yet to give much back. I hope in whatever years are left to me, I can begin to give something back in return for all the love I have received."

Very Russian, very, very Russian. Your Russian cannot celebrate without slobbering into tears. The Irish laugh at death, the Russians weep over it.

Peter was next.

"We are grateful to God for sending us Tatiana Alekseevna and for her energy and enthusiasm and deep faith. She shows all the young people who meet her that in the new Russia, faith and intelligence and talent can and will be combined."

"And she is so sweet and good with the little children," his wife added.

Father O'Brien would certainly do better.

"This reminds me just a little bit of a retirement party for a priest here in Boston, when in fact it is a coming-to-adulthood party for an extraordinarily gifted and generous young woman. Odessa, to use the name I am more familiar with, I toast the many happy years that are ahead of you and all the good you will do for those you love."

Yeah.

"Ivan . . ." Father Peter looked at me.

Oh, oh! I was supposed to say something. Flanigan you are a real jerk. Why didn't you see that coming? I'd have to sing. Panic surged through me as it usually does before a performance. Then whatever it is that clicks in the back of my head when I learn how to mimic an accent or am trying to sink a putt or am about to perform, clicked.

I hummed the melody from the opera *Eugene Onegin*, based on Pushkin's masterpiece. Tatiana looked up in surprise and began to blush.

I outdid the tenor who had sung it on the stage of the Lyric Opera in Chicago. I bowed and scraped and gestured and floated around the room as I sang the hymn to Tatiana, albeit another one, and this time in English instead of French.

> *Come let us celebrate, congratulate*
> *Our lovely lady on this day*
> *Her sweet and charming ways*
> *Bring joy to all our days*
> *And so may it always be*
> *Long may you shine, beautiful Tatiana!*
> *Long may you shine, beautiful Tatiana!*
>
> *May fortune always give joy*
> *to each day she lives*
> *On her may life ever smile*
> *Let her life be like a star*
> *Shining always from afar*
> *Lighting our night and day!*
> *Long may you shine, beautiful Tatiana!*
> *Long may you shine, beautiful Tatiana!*

The assembly joined in the final refrain.

"Oh, sing it again, *please!*" Annah begged.

"Gladly," I said and began again. This time they joined me in the refrain. Tatiana sobbed (naturally, she was Russian) and blushed furiously when

I lifted her chin so I could stare into her over-flowing brown eyes.

I was on a roll, a dangerous condition for me to be in.

At the end of the second rendition, I raised my vodka glass and said triumphantly, "Tatiana Alekseevna, our bright morning star!"

The rest of the guests joined the cry. The three Russians downed their "one glass vodka" in a single gulp. Father O'Brien and I sipped ours much more discreetly.

"Onegin," Tatiana said to me, her face now glowing with gratitude. "Second act. How wonderful of you, Ivan."

"In French, as I remember it," Father O'Brien added.

"Now I make tea and we eat sandwiches and cake."

The company relaxed and we had a delightful time at the birthday party. Why two priests, a priest's wife, and an unlikely redhead from Boston College? Surely she had more friends. Yet perhaps she was poor compared to most Harvard types and lonely. She could only celebrate with those who shared intense faith with her—which was giving me more credit than I deserved.

Despite my good intentions, I managed to find a seat on an ottoman from which I had a clear view of the nude. It was her, all right, and doubtless a clinically accurate sketch, if modestly cautious. But she did not see through herself the way she had seen through me.

I persuaded them to sample my raspberry Frango mints. Everyone rolled their eyes in appreciation, as well they might. The birthday queen helped herself to a second. I would order another shipment when I got back to B.C.—if I ever made it back.

Father O'Brien and I left together.

"Are you all right, Jack?" he asked me after I had stumbled for the third time on the steps.

Since the rain has stopped I could not plead slippery steps.

"One glass vodka is one glass too many for me, Father. I'm a short hitter."

"Nonetheless, I think the Irish covered themselves with glory this afternoon. That was a wonderful tribute to her and brilliantly sung. It just about broke the poor kid's heart. . . . I couldn't believe it when she said that there was an Irish young man coming to lunch."

"And especially one who is a classic type."

"I'm not so sure about that. . . . You put your finger on what she is, you know, a morning star, a bright star which shines on all who know her. I don't think I've ever met anyone with faith like that. Yet she is hardly a monastic type, do you think?"

"Russian mysticism is incredibly varied, Father," I said. "Not all of it monastic by any means. Some of the greatest of their mystics were married men and women with families, much more of them than in our heritage."

"I hoped you'd say that."

Insofar as I was capable of rational thought, I wondered all the way back to Chestnut Hill on the MBTA what the priest had meant by that.

A more frightening thought occurred to me as I hiked to my room: Odessa figured that God was leaning over backward to take charge of her life. Had she decided that Prince Ivan the Red had been sent by God to take care of her?

Nonsense!

God wouldn't send me to take care of anyone. Would He?

But what if He had?

CHAPTER

2

There was more family trouble waiting for me back at B.C. This time it was a call from my brother Edward, or Junior, as Dad often called him.

If Dad is a jerk, though a well-meaning one, Ed is a prig and not often a well-meaning prig. He's a big handsome guy like Dad. From the day of his birth, Dad had assumed that Junior would follow him into surgery. What else could he possibly want to do? Ed had decided, however, that he wanted to do something to "help" people, so he choose social work as a profession. You can imagine what that choice and its accompanying argument did to Dad.

How could anyone help other human beings better than by cutting them open?

I can understand why Ed's sense of his own worth required him to oppose Dad on every possible occasion. Unfortunately, Ed's ego required that he try to engage in rational discussion with Dad on all imaginable subjects. This was crazy. You didn't discuss with Dad, you didn't try to argue with him, you didn't engage in sweet reasoning. You shouted him down and ignored him. Sometimes he even changed his mind, though he'd never admit it.

Ed's wife Maria was Italian, no, worse—Sicilian— in Dad's terminology a "wop" or a "dago." The proper answer to that would have been to call him a shanty Irish bigot and tell him you intended to marry the woman whether he liked her or not. But not our Ed. He tried to make a serious case that Italians were better wives and mothers than Irish women.

Did Ed fall in love with Maria merely to spite Dad? I wouldn't have put it past him. He'd been more lucky than he deserved. She was a wonderful woman. Dad didn't call her a "wop" to her face, but he left no doubt that he regarded her as some sort of inferior human being. Maria responded by hating him with a passion that only

Sicilians can muster when they decide to hate someone.

Oddly perhaps, but not untypically, Dad has come to admire her skills as a mother and even, I think, to like her. He would never say that to her, of course, and certainly never apologize for being a jerk. But now, five years and two children into the marriage, he has become genuinely fond of her. Too late: She will neither forgive nor forget.

"Face it, Maria," I had said to her, "the asshole is fond of you. Smile at him and you'll own him."

"He is a fool," she replied, spitting the words out. "I do not want to live in the same neighborhood with him."

With the income from his trust fund—grandfather Mahoney had set one up for each of us—Ed had bought a home in the neighborhood so, it seemed in my admittedly cynical opinion, he could punish Dad constantly by his presence and engage in acrimonious ideological arguments.

You can imagine what Christmas is like at our house.

And it's up to me, the harmless lower middle child, to be the mediator and the healer. That's how bad things are.

My techniques are varied, everything from quiet

conversations with Maria and even with Stephanie's idiot husband Joe to a loud demand, "Would you clowns knock it off so I can enjoy Christmas!"

Generally what I do doesn't work.

I'm also the one that the others talk to when they're unhappy, which is usually. Even when I'm in Russia, they track me down with their tales of woe.

Why don't they go to Mom?

You don't go to a professional litigator with your family problems. She always takes the other guy's side and wants to cross-examine you.

So John Mahoney Flanigan, supremely unqualified for mediation, is *faut de mieux*, the blessed peacemaker who gets shot at from both sides.

Mom insists that it is my wit and humor that grease the wheels of family relationships and make them turn more smoothly. I think she means that no one in the family hates me much, arguably because I am generally so inconsequential as not to merit hate.

Anyway, Ed was on the phone that evening worried about Brigid.

"I think it is your moral obligation to have a long talk with Brigid, Jack."

Get it? Everything is a moral obligation.

"Brigie's fine," I reply.

"I don't think so."

"What do you think is wrong?"

"I am convinced that she's smoking *pot*!"

"So what?"

"Do you know the dangers in smoking pot?"

"More or less."

"She is risking her future happiness, perhaps even her life."

"You smoked pot, didn't you, Ed?"

"Certainly. I didn't know then how dangerous it could be."

"Dad knew the research. Didn't he tell you that it could be dangerous?"

"That was different."

"Yeah? How?"

Pause while his agile mind searched for an answer, one that would satisfy a University of Chicago intellectual, as he thought of himself.

"That was across generation lines. You can speak to Brigid from within her own generation."

"In Brigie's view anyone over twenty is in the older generation."

"That's what Maria tells me."

"Then I guess I'm right."

"Nonetheless, Brigid trusts you. You have a moral obligation. . . ."

"You know, Junior, as you get older you become more like the old man. You're going to be as tough on your kids as he was on you and Steph. And the kids will stick it to you just as you and Steph did to Dad."

Dead silence.

"Maria said that too?"

"As a matter of fact, she did. Apples, she insists, don't fall very far from their trees. . . ."

A brilliantly original insight. I had to get rid of him if I were to finish that night my political science paper on the advantages of political machines.

"Look, Brigie has her head screwed on right, no thanks to the rest of the family. She's probably the sanest teenager we've produced yet. If she's using pot at all, it's episodic. She's too smart to fry her brains. I'll have a word or two with her sometime soon when it seems natural to bring the subject up."

"I knew you'd see things my way. Remember, Jack, her whole future may depend on how you handle this problem."

"Yeah."

See things his way? I'd never in all my life seen things his way, except on the subject of Maria, and he'd probably fallen in love with her for the wrong reasons.

Moreover, Maria had the good taste to like me. Well, at least to laugh at my jokes.

Moreover, as a doctoral candidate in Social Service Administration, he should have realized that his conversation with me was a crock of excrement.

If I moved back to Chicago, I would settle on the far opposite end of the city, up near Evanston, although that is a shocking statement from a South Sider.

If they called me in Boston, not to say Moscow, with their goofiness, greater distances than Evanston would never be enough protection.

So I finished the paper and decided that I simply wouldn't show up next Tuesday at the bench on the edge of Harvard Square. I had enough problems as it was.

Despite the cold northeastern breeze and the threat of more rain, the kids were there again on Tuesday listening to a new story. Ivan the Red had become Ivan the Nice, though as far as I could tell he was as inept as ever. The kids giggled and stole furtive glances at me whenever Ivan the Nice did or said something stupid, especially the little girls.

"You do not have to come every day," she said to me as we crossed the street. "I don't want you to feel obligated."

"Hey," I said, "you don't need practice in speaking English. I'm the one who needs practice in speaking Russian."

"That is true."

When a woman tells you that she is making no claims on you, it is always the case that she has just increased the level of the claims.

"You go to the symphony ever?"

"I cannot afford the tickets."

"I managed to find two tickets for tomorrow night. We could have dinner before."

"I do not know. . . ."

"Tchaikovsky."

"I will embarrass you. I will weep all evening."

"All Russians weep when they hear Pyotr Il-lyich."

"That is true too. . . ."

She sounded honestly hesitant. Was she going to turn me down?

"I am being very foolish, Ivan the Nice. I would love to accompany you to the symphony."

"Great!" I said enthusiastically. "I'll pick you up at—"

"That will not be necessary. I will meet you in front of Symphony Hall. Fifteen minutes before the concert begins."

"Six o'clock at the Budapest Restaurant in the Copley Square Hotel. Hungarian food. We'll walk down Huntington to Symphony Hall."

"Very well."

So we reached an important milestone in our relationship. We were about to embark on our first authentic date.

"Sorry I gave you so little warning. I realized only yesterday that it was an all-Russian night."

That was not altogether true. I'd realized it on Friday morning. I'd agonized through the weekend about whether I wanted to take her on a real date.

"That is not a problem."

Maybe she'd be a creep on a real date. Then all my problems would be solved.

She wasn't a creep. Underneath her worn cloth coat she was wearing a charcoal gray turtleneck dress which clung to her in such an ingenious fashion that by definition she could not be a creep. Her hair was back in its ponytail. Her mother's jewels were in their usual places. Her lips were, if anything, marginally more colorful than they had been at her birthday party.

Dazzling. Ravishing.

"You look beautiful tonight, Odessa. The dress is perfect for you."

"Thank you," she said with a deep blush, "Ivan the Nice."

Those who looked at us, which was everyone in the wood-paneled restaurant with stained glass windows and red leather chairs, surely wondered what the grand duchess could see in the punk with the red hair.

Fair question.

She even agreed to drink "one glass red wine" with our Hungarian goulash.

"This is a date?" she asked me as the bottle of wine appeared.

"I think so. A real date."

"Then do we talk English or Russian?"

"Whatever you wish."

"Perhaps English? This not a class exercise, is it?"

Only if I were even worse a fool than I usually am.

"Not exactly . . . English it will be."

The dress was new and certainly didn't cost more than fifty dollars. Perfect fit. Good taste. By no means what one could reasonably expect from a Russian.

"You were fascinated with my self-portrait at the party," she said, an observation not an accusation.

"I'm a male member of the species with the normal hormones, maybe a little above normal," I said gently, for this was a matter that required gentleness. "Naked women, or should I say nude women, fascinate me, especially when their bodies are as sumptuous as the one in the portrait."

She tilted her head and blushed.

"You embarrass me, Ivan."

"Did I seem disrespectful when I gawked at the young woman in the picture?"

"No. Not at all . . . you really did find me pleasing?"

"The woman in the picture is gorgeous. Any man would be interested in her. It's not you, but that's all right."

"Not me?"

I tasted the merlot as if I could tell whether it were good or bad. I nodded approvingly at the wine steward. He poured it into the ruby red goblets that are part of the Budapest's atmosphere.

"Oh, no. The sketch has your beauty and modesty, but neither your fragility nor your strength. When you sketched me, you saw right through me. You don't see through yourself yet, which isn't surprising. Takes time."

She tilted her head again. "I must try harder."

"Maybe you should wait till you see yourself in the eyes of a man who knows you and all your faults and loves you."

"You are very wise, Ivan. As always."

"Do I get the sketch?"

"Certainly not!" she exclaimed, blushing again.

"Didn't think I would."

She changed the subject to the composer of the evening. The poor man was forced to marry, though he was obviously gay. Russians were not tolerant of sexual diversity then, not that they are tolerant now. Many Americans are not tolerant either. But they are not as bad as Russians. After all the years of socialism Russians needed much grace from God to accept diversity. They are terrible haters.

"You should see my family," I replied.

"Did you send my sketch to your mother?"

"Sure did. Haven't heard from her yet."

Lie, but only a white lie. I had put it on my desk, half intending, as the Irish would say, to throw it in the mail. Now to keep my white lie from becoming something worse I would have to send it off first thing in the morning. Mom was on the board of the Art Institute. She would be candid in her reaction. She didn't know how to be anything else.

As advertised, Odessa wept through the whole concert, though not loud enough to embarrass me. She also clung to my hand, which was a pleasant diversion.

"You wept for Russia?" I asked her as a cab took us back to Cambridge. She was still holding my hand. I was not about to repudiate that gesture.

She sighed.

"For Holy Russia which has suffered so much."

"But whose suffering will save the world?"

"I am not so much a romantic fool, Ivan the Sweet, as to believe that."

Ivan the Sweet, huh? I was progressing. But in the stories I would still be an inept bungler.

She had protested that it was not necessary to

take a cab or for me to escort her home. I had insisted that I would be in great trouble if my mother ever found out that I had not.

"It has been a very nice date," she said. "You need not come up the steps with me."

"I'm not about to try to come in with you, Odessa," I replied.

I heard the humming sound again.

"I know that, Ivan. If I were so silly as to invite you in, you wouldn't accept my invitation."

"Don't be so sure about that."

"I am sure."

"I have, ah, four tickets for next week. Thursday. Mozart. I'm inviting two friends from B.C. I hope you can join us."

"They will approve of me?"

That's what I wanted to find out, but it was not fair for her to ask.

"They have excellent taste, so I'm sure they will."

"I will be happy to accompany you. I promise you not to weep during Mozart. Rather I will laugh often, as one should when listening to Mozart."

I was now agonizing, like a fifteen-year-old, over whether I should kiss her good night.

She solved the problem by kissing me. It was not

a passionate, lingering kiss, not by a long shot. But it was not merely a platonic peck either. Rather it was sweet, affectionate, and grateful.

"I have enjoyed the evening very much, Ivan. Thank you."

I was so shaken by the kiss that I don't think I said anything, except maybe "see you tomorrow morning."

I must have taken the MBTA back to Chestnut Hill, but I have no recollection of that. I seemed to float on a soft and luxurious cloud.

It wasn't that great a kiss.

Well, maybe it was.

Mom called me on Friday morning.

"Are you having an affair with that woman?"

That's how litigators begin conversations.

"Mom, you know I don't have affairs . . . and what woman?"

"The one who did that sketch."

"What makes you think it was a woman?"

"Only a woman could see through you that way."

"Yeah?"

"Who is she?"

"Harvard," I replied, hoping there was a tone of disdain in my voice.

"Are you having a romance with her?"

"Objection."

"Overruled. Answer the question."

"I wouldn't call it that."

"All right. Let me rephrase the question. Are you dating her?"

"Took her to the symphony one night."

"She's very, very good. You know that, don't you, Jack?"

"I kind of thought she was."

"And she cares deeply about you."

"I'm not so sure about that."

"Depend on it, she does. . . . Would I like her?"

"Perhaps. . . . How's the old fella doing?"

"About the same. You know what he's like. Sometimes I think he's mellowing and sometimes I think I am. . . . Brigie is after me to get a divorce."

She laughed at the suggestion, dismissing it as an absurdity.

"Brigie's problem is that she thinks she understands everything and only half does."

"That's very perceptive, Jack."

Maybe she did still love the jerk. Maybe she knew he was a jerk when she married him. Maybe she didn't care then and still didn't care.

"He's going off to Bosnia again for two weeks.

I think he was never happier than when he was stitching people together in 'Nam."

"That's very generous of him."

"No one ever said he wasn't generous. . . . Now when do I get to meet this woman?"

"I'm not sure you will."

"How old is she?"

"Just turned twenty-one."

"You give her a birthday present?"

"Yep."

"What?"

"Objection."

"Overruled."

"A box of raspberry Frango mints."

"The last of the big-time spenders . . . remember what I said, Jack. She's good, and she's at least half in love with you."

"I doubt it," I said uneasily.

"Is she Catholic?"

The question still mattered. Maybe it always would.

"Orthodox."

"Jewish?"

"Russian Orthodox, but she goes to St. Paul's, the Catholic Church here."

"Good. . . . Tell her I said that she was very good and that she's half in love with you."

"I'll tell her the first anyway. . . . How's Brigie?"

"In open revolt, even when she can't find something to revolt about. I hope she grows up."

"She will."

"She's too damn good-looking for her own good."

"Like her mother."

She laughed and hung up.

On the following Tuesday, after the little kids had heard about Ivan the Sweet (predictably still a bungler, however sweet he might be) and we settled in at our restaurant for lunch, I told Odessa that my mother liked the sketch and said that she was a very gifted artist.

"Did she really?"

"Yep. Mom isn't the type that praises easily. If she said it, she meant it. Moreover she's on the board of the Art Institute, so she knows what she's talking about."

Tears welled up in her luscious brown eyes. "Tell her I said thank you."

"I will."

"Ivan, there are so many things to do. Sometimes I don't know which way to turn."

"If you really believe that you're caught up in the fullness of God's love, like you say, you'd trust in Her direction."

"You're right, of course," she said dabbing at her tears with a piece of tissue. "It is so difficult to remember that all the time. But I permit myself to be distracted from the making of tea."

"Have you dated often since you came to Harvard?" I asked her, a question which plainly was none of my business.

"Not often," she said, handing me my tea cup with the usual bow. "I have been very busy learning English and studying for my classes and working at the Russian Center and running in the morning and praying. There has been little time for a social life."

Our tear fest at the symphony was no doubt her first real date in this country. I was prudent enough not to say that.

"Now you have time?"

"It would seem so. Perhaps I worry less about my studies. I know my grades will enable me to go to graduate school wherever I want."

"And you want?"

"Harvard perhaps. Or Berkeley. Or San Diego or Chicago."

Ah. Now wasn't that interesting.

"Art history?"

"Perhaps. Probably."

"At Chicago you could also perhaps have artistic training at the Art Institute. Where my mother is on the board."

"Yes?"

"Yes."

"Perhaps."

I was getting way ahead of myself. At that point I didn't want my family to meet Odessa or her to meet my family.

"Why don't you paint in oils? The painting of your mother is wonderful."

"Oils cost too much."

"Good reason."

Actually a bad reason, but it opened up the possibility of a Christmas present. If I were still seeing her at Christmas.

"What was your Easter experience like, the one that made you a Christian again?"

She lifted her shoulder.

"Commonplace. Friends of mine who were Christian took me to a small church in a Moscow neighborhood. I listened to the Easter Alleluia. It was lovely. Then suddenly time stood still. The whole world seemed to invade me. I was filled with joy and laughter and love, oh, so much love. I knew everything would be all right. I saw that the world was filled with love and I was part of that love. It was unbearable and wonderful and very brief. It was long enough, however. So afterwards when they said to me the traditional Easter greeting, 'Christ is risen, Alleluia!' and I replied, 'He is risen indeed, Alleluia!' I knew that the greeting was true, the most true thing I would ever hear."

At the memory tears flooded into her eyes.

"It hasn't happened again?"

"Oh, yes, Ivan. It happens often. Even when I don't want it to happen. The Risen Lord fills me like a lover would. I am exhausted but unbearably happy."

Yeah?

"Do you think you will go to a monastery and become a nun?"

"Perhaps. Perhaps not. If I were to be a nun, why should I come here and study so hard? I think He has other plans for me."

Including marriage? No you idiot, don't ask that question.

She answered it for me.

"Sometimes I think I should marry. That seems

to be what God wants of me. I am not certain, however. I tell Him that he must send the right lover."

Yikes!

"Jesus wouldn't object to a rival?"

She dismissed my question with a wave of her hand.

"God considers a spouse to be an ally rather than a rival."

Well, that settles that. I didn't pursue the subject.

My friend Michael is a good man, even if he is from Boston. So is my friend Megan a good woman, even if she too is from Boston. I would not say that they are a couple exactly. They are remarkably skillful at the bobbing-and-weaving-and-teasing-and-avoiding-romantic-commitment game which I think the Irish invented. They were delighted at my invitation to the Mozart concert and astonished to learn that I would bring a date.

We drove into Cambridge in Michael's new Pontiac.

"You don't really have a date, do you, Jack?" Megan demanded. "Not a real date?"

"There's a young woman who said she'd come to the concert with me."

"Have you taken her out before?"

"Once."

"What's she like?"

"She's nice."

"You're no help at all!"

"She good looking?" Michael asked.

"You'll have to be the judge of that."

"She's Irish of course," Megan continued the game, "isn't she?"

"Russian."

"Russian!"

"Yep. Russian."

"What's her name?"

"She has two names—Odessa and Tatiana."

"Mysterious?"

"Filled with mystery."

"I can hardly wait to meet her. . . . Will I like her, Jack?"

"Perhaps."

They would adore her, but I wasn't going to tell them that. Meg, true to the loyalties of her gender, would take Odessa's side against me.

She opened the door when I knocked.

"Do I appear appropriate, Ivan?" she asked in Russian. "I do not want to embarrass you with your friends."

She was wearing the beige suit from her birthday party, now with a light blue sweater, defying, I thought, the harsh November weather.

"You would never embarrass anyone, Odessa." I said helping her on with her coat. "And you look totally lovely."

"Perhaps."

My friends gulped audibly when I opened the car door for her. Even in her old and shapeless coat, Odessa's exotic beauty was evident.

Will she sit quietly in the backseat, I wondered.

Silly question.

She chatted amiably with my friends, talking without hesitation about growing up in Russia, about her studies, her work at the Russian Center, and her plans for graduate school. I learned for the first time that she had spent time in Warsaw and Berlin when her father was stationed in the West.

The only hint of mysticism was her comment that her parents were both happy with God.

My friends believed in God. After all, they were Irish Catholics, weren't they?

But, like the rest of us from that unusual subspecies, they normally spoke about God only at wakes, and then cautiously.

Odessa got away with it because she had charmed both of them. And they had yet to see her with the coat off.

When they did in the Rialto Restaurant in the Charles Hotel, they gulped again. I felt kind of proud. With no rational grounds for being proud.

"Why do you call Jack Ivan?" Megan asked when we were seated at our table.

"That is Russian for John. We speak Russian usually. I help him, though he is very good at it."

"Does he pay you?" Megan demanded.

"Oh, no. He is very amusing. That is enough."

"Sounds like exploitation to me."

"He did give me some wonderful chocolate raspberry candy for my birthday."

"Cheapskate!"

"Have you ever thought," Odessa said, deftly changing the subject as the waiter served our Provençal fisherman's soup, "what the world would be like without music?"

Naturally none of us had.

"We would still be humans and life would go on, but it would be much more difficult to mourn our losses and celebrate our loves. God gave us music, I think, so that we would have some hint of what She is like. God sings to our hearts with music, telling us of love about which we would know much less if it were not for music."

"That's very interesting," Michael said. "I never thought of it that way."

"Even rock music, which is not to my taste, tells us something about God."

"So God must be especially proud of Mozart?" Megan asked cautiously.

"Oh, yes. The poor man suffered so much."

"Does that go with being gifted?"

"Perhaps. For some people."

So it went. We drove across the Charles River at the Harvard Bridge and turned right on Storrow Drive, which we would take to Mass. Avenue.

The night was crisp and clear. The full moon, just rising from the harbor, hung ahead of us. It bathed the river in glittering, dappled splendor.

"See how the moon turns the river radiant," Odessa told us, "just as the eyes of the lover turn the face and body of the beloved radiant with love."

None of us said anything about that. How could we?

She held my hand during the concert, though there was no need to weep at Mozart.

"Do you Russians believe that sex gets in the way of God?" Michael asked at intermission.

"Oh, no," Odessa replied promptly. "Anything can get in the way of God, greed, lust, envy, pride. But sexual love when it's really love tells us what God is like. God, you see, is an aroused lover. All the time. Also a very patient lover with a wonderful sense of humor, as you Americans would say."

"I never heard it put that way," Megan said thoughtfully.

"That's how God describes himself in the sacred scriptures. You know the Song of Solomon, of course?"

They didn't, but they weren't prepared to admit it.

Odessa quoted a chapter from memory, in a translation I had never heard, which was, to say the least, candid.

She examined our shocked faces carefully.

"It surprises you?"

"Not at all," Meg said. "It is very beautiful."

As we were going back into the concert hall, Meg whispered to me, "That's in the bible? The Catholic bible too?"

"Sure," I responded, like I knew what I was talking about.

Summer Road was our first stop on the way home. I escorted my date up the stairs. Too quick a return would land me in serious trouble with Megan. Besides it was my turn to initiate the kissing.

"Your friends are such good people, Ivan," she said. "I knew they would be. It was a wonderful evening."

"It sure was. I told you that they'd like you, didn't I?"

"Yes."

The rain had stopped, but it was bitter cold.

I took her face in my hands and drew it towards my own. She gulped.

I caressed her cheeks lightly and then kissed her several times gently, teasingly. She gulped again. My final act was a firm and vigorous kiss, not a mouth lock, heaven knows, and not terribly passionate. Rather it was a challenging, demanding, loving (I hoped) kiss. She replied in kind.

We moved apart, she with a sigh.

"You are a very good kisser, Ivan Eduardovich."

"I hope respectful."

The hum that passed for a laugh.

"Of course. Very respectful. But not dull."

I think I floated down the stairs to face the catechism which awaited me during our ride back to Chestnut Hill.

"Are you sleeping with her, Jack?" Meg, naturally, was the one to ask that inevitable question.

"Certainly not."

"Are you in love with her?"

"Not yet."

"She's in love with you, I hope you know that?"

"Is she?"

"Do you think you might marry her?"

"Much too early to say."

"Don't you dare hurt her, do you hear?"

"I won't."

"I can't believe that a woman like her actually thinks you're special." Michael joined in the conversation.

"Neither can I . . . but, face it, she is kind of strange."

"Strange!" Megan exploded.

"That kind of Asian face, no expressions, the religion stuff."

"It's a wonderfully expressive face," Megan said hotly. "You just have to watch the cues, especially when she looks at you."

That's what I was afraid of.

"Really . . . and I think she's numinous."

"You mean luminous?" Michael asked.

"*No!* I mean numinous. Kind of like the transcendent, whatever that is, is present in her. Most people couldn't get away with talking about God that way. She does it without being offensive because she really believes it. She makes God exciting."

"I'm sure God is delighted."

"Promise me that you'll be nice to her."

"Wasn't I nice to her tonight?"

"Kind of. . . . Promise me you'll never hurt her!"

"If I did, I think I'd be in deep trouble with God."

"You'd better believe it."

Sleep came slowly that night. I was on the slippery slope. If I kept sliding down it, the result would be love, marriage, children, family.

My older siblings had made a mess out of that process. Ed had lucked out through no fault of his own. Steph? Ugh. They both were fighting Dad. Maybe Mom too. Terrible thing to put your life in jeopardy just to punish your parents.

Was Odessa a punishment I intended to inflict on my parents?

They would probably react to Odessa, each in their own way, as Michael and Megan had.

I had nothing against marriage and family. I was, however, in no rush. There were a lot of things to be done before I turned domestic. Right?

Why not do them with a woman you love?

Well, it would be harder.

Why couldn't God have sent me to take care of Odessa, if that's what She had in mind, when I was, say, twenty-six or twenty-seven?

You take your true love whenever she comes along, regardless of your age or the time in your life. Right?

Was Odessa my true love?

That was a question designed to keep me awake till morning. I'd better face it now, while there was still time to get off the slippery slope.

I decided that as exotic and as lovely and as fascinating as she was, she could not be my true love. Her background was so different from mine. Right?

That decision made, I relaxed and permitted the sleep of the just man to overtake me.

I felt thoroughly rotten about it the next morning. My feelings were not helped when I encountered Megan on my way to the MTBA.

"She's absolutely charming," that worthy insisted. "Do you know how lucky you are?"

"Perhaps," I said.

All the way in on the train and through my class I felt sorry for myself. Yet I had to end the relationship at lunch today. Otherwise I'd end up hurting her. Right?

My resolution lasted till I found my way to our rendezvous bench. The little kids were dressed up in snow suits. Late November. It wasn't that cold, was it?

This morning Prince Ivan had become Prince Ivan the Wonderful. He even managed to make one or two minor contributions to the work of Vasilisa the Wise and Baba Yaga.

When they and their mothers departed and we stood up to walk across the street, Odessa kissed me, a light brushing of lips, as though that was the way we always greeted one another in public.

"I overslept," she confessed in Russian, "and had to run before I came over there. I hope I don't embarrass you at lunch in my running clothes."

"It is inconceivable that you could ever embarrass me, Tatiana Alekseevna."

So I slid further down the slippery slope.

She kissed me goodbye after lunch. I arranged to pick her up on Friday to see the *Michael Collins* film.

So this is what being in love is like? An interesting experience. I now had no choice but to play out the relationship to the end, no matter what the end was.

Then, heaven help me, I spent most of the time on the ride back fantasizing about Odessa in bed. I was a very tender and gentle lover. Yet she would be too much for me. Wouldn't she?

Dad was on the phone almost as soon as I was back in my room.

"We're having more trouble with Stephanie, Jack," he said, outraged as he always is when he's complaining about his children.

"So what else is new."

"She's trying to break the trust fund so she can get at the capital."

"I'm sure Big John Mahoney made it unbreakable."

"That's what your mother said. . . . Steph can't live the lifestyle she wants out of the income. That jerk that got her pregnant again can't hold a job. So she needs more money."

"Don't give it to her," I said. "Don't buy her off, Dad. That won't help at all."

"Yeah, that's what your mother says."

"So I'm clearly right."

"He's a substitute high school teacher now. Can you imagine that? A Notre Dame degree and he's a high school teacher. And a substitute at that."

Joe Devine, Steph's husband, was bright enough. Unfortunately he had illusions that he was both a writer and an actor. Even more unfortunately, he had not the slightest talent in either area.

"They both have to grow up," I insisted.

"That's what your mother says."

"So?"

"I'm going off to Bosnia tomorrow. A team of us. Some of the best surgeons in the country. We have to do it."

"That's very generous."

"Well, I don't know about that. Stephanie says I'm stingy."

"Steph lies."

"I suppose so. . . . Anyway, I wanted to say good-bye to you, just in case anything happens."

I felt a chill in the pit of my stomach.

"Be careful, Dad."

"Yeah, I will. No real danger. Steph really upsets me, you know that."

"She's manipulated you all her life, Dad. She's got to find out that it doesn't play any more."

"That's what your mother says."

Dad was a jerk, a loudmouth jerk. But no one ever said he was not generous.

The trust funds Big John had left for the four of us were impressive. That was how I'd managed to travel to Russia for three summers. I figured that I could live comfortably as a single man off the income for the rest of my life. As a supplement to a regular job, it would be the difference between comfort and luxury.

Big John, a redhead like Brigie and me, was as colorful an Irish pirate as Chicago had ever seen. Real estate, commodities, trucking, automobiles, he did it all with flair and success and generosity. Moreover, as Mom had often said, he never came close to an indictment.

He and Dad had hit it off well. He loved to pull Dad's leg about doctors and especially about surgeons. Dad did not seem to mind. I got along with Dad because I followed Granddad's script.

If Dad were a jerk, and Junior a prig, and Mom a litigator, Steph was a flake, a spoiled lazy flake. She expected the whole world would fall on its face in front of her because she was beautiful, without her ever having to do any work. She wasn't dumb, but as Brigie had said, she was worse: *boring*!

"Jack, she, like, never reads anything. I mean, she's totally illiterate."

She flunked out of St. Mary's of Notre Dame

after her first year because her social life had interfered with her education. Dad used all his considerable clout to get her back into school. She flunked out again, but not before she had seduced Joe Devine, a hapless innocent who hung around the drama department at St. Mary's.

I had seen him in one of his plays. I was maybe thirteen, but I could see that he was without talent.

Dad had been furious. There had never been a shotgun marriage before. Joe was a cad and a heel and a coward. No good would come of such a marriage.

They got married anyway.

There *had* been shotgun marriages in the family before. Indeed if Dad had ever looked at his own baptismal certificate (as I had) he would have noted that his surgeon father and the nurse who was his mother had been married five months before he was born. I kept that information to myself.

The marriage was in trouble from day one. They lived in Minneapolis where Joe hung around the Guthrie Theater doing unpaid odds and ends and hoping for his "big break," a break that could never come. Steph on the one hand was impatient with him for not fighting hard enough against those who denied him the break to which she figured he was entitled, and on the other hand upset that he was not bringing in a steady income.

So now he was a high school teacher, a profession at which he probably excelled. They had two children and a third on the way. She probably wanted more money so she could dump him and start over with someone more reliable.

"She'd divorce him," Mom had once assured me, "if she thought we'd take her back and guarantee the good life for her. Your father thinks we should."

"And you say?"

"No way. Make her grow up."

"Can she grow up, Mom?"

"I'm not sure."

So that was where the matter stood. They'd be home for Christmas, Steph sulking and Joe a confused, troubled hangdog.

Ugh.

Brigie was the next one on the phone. She began as she always did, spoiling for a fight.

"*Well,* I suppose you've been talking to Eddie, that asshole."

"He's been talking to me."

"*And* I suppose he'd been telling you that I'm heavy into pot."

"Something like that."

"*And* he wants you to talk to me about it."

"That was the implication."

To put it mildly.

"I *suppose* he told you it was your moral obligation."

"I believe those words were used."

"*So* why haven't you talked to me about frying my brains?"

"Because I didn't believe him."

"You didn't?"

The wind went out of her sails.

"Certainly not. I figured you might have tried it once or twice but that you were too smart to fry your brains like he almost did when he was your age."

"Oh," she said in a tiny voice.

"Should I talk to you about it?"

"Jack, I've smoked pot exactly twice and I hated it. It makes me sick. I'll never do it again."

"I figured."

"Why does everyone have to think the worst about me?"

"I don't."

"That's true. . . . You heard that Dad is going to Bosnia again? Isn't that crazy?"

"Or brave."

"He did his part in Vietnam."

"No one ever said that he wasn't generous. Maybe too generous."

"You heard about Steph?"

"Yep."

"Isn't she a terrible fool?"

"Yep."

"And Joe is not a bad guy."

"No, he's not."

"Is everyone afraid that I'm going to do the same thing?"

"I'm not."

"Why not?"

"Because you may be a brat on occasion, but you've never been a spoiled brat."

"I guess not."

Why should I be a parent to a teenage girl? Woman. Whatever . . .

"When do I get to meet her?"

"Who?"

"Whom . . . the woman who did that sketch of you."

"It's not that serious, Brigid."

"I bet it is. Will I like her?"

"Most people do."

"Bitchin' . . . Bring her home for Christmas!"

"To our house?"

"Yeah, I guess you're right."

All I needed now was a call from Stephanie. Not very likely. She was the only one in the family who truly hated me.

On Friday night, after the movie, while we were consuming our malted milks (which they don't make on the East Coast like they do in Chicago), I told Odessa about my family.

She had held my hand during the film—which disturbed her deeply—and my hand had found its way to her jean-covered knee.

"Is it not wonderful," she commented, "how they all trust you? Are you not kind of a priest for the rest of them?"

"Except for Steph . . . yeah, well I never looked on it that way. Maybe you have a point. I never applied for the job."

"Have you ever thought of becoming a priest, Ivan? You'd be a wonderful priest."

"Yeah, I've thought about it. Not the way the Church is fouled up now. I don't think it's my way, not even if the Church wasn't run by fools."

So I put that fear of hers to rest.

I showed her our family picture.

"I don't know why I carry it around in my wallet. They drive me crazy."

"Because you love them. . . . My, what a handsome group."

"Except for me."

She waved that exercise in self-pity aside.

"The child with the red hair is the one who carries the name of the sun goddess?"

"Yep, that's Brigie."

"She is very beautiful. How fortunate she is to have you to take care of her. God has been good to her."

"If you say so."

"Perhaps they will all improve."

"Then the age of miracles will not be over."

She handed the picture back to me.

"I will pray for them every day."

"And for me."

"Oh, I already do that."

So we continued our cautious dance, two noontime conversations in Russian every week and some kind of date or quasi-date once a week.

My kisses grew somewhat more passionate. She didn't seem to mind.

I didn't go home on Thanksgiving. It was not a big feast day for her, but I took her to dinner that night anyway.

The slope got slipperier.

I took her over to Boston College when we **played** the Fighting Baptists from Notre Dame. She knew enough about football from the television not to be too confused by it. It was a bitter cold day. She shivered through the second half, so I had to cuddle her in my arms.

Why would a Russian shiver on a late November day in America? Hadn't she known a lot worse weather at home?

She hadn't been home for a couple of years, had she?

I don't know whether I warmed her up much. However, she certainly did warm me up.

Megan and Michael took us out to supper. We had a grand time. Odessa seemed very happy.

I guess I did too.

She talked at great length about how the Russians celebrated Christmas. The Socialist regime tried to suppress it completely and then transferred the celebration to New Year's Day. Now most people were again celebrating on the day of "our Lord and Savior's birth, which is when it should be celebrated."

"What do you do on Christmas, Tatiana?" Megan asked.

I could see it coming.

"Not very much. I go to the midnight worship at St. Paul's and shock poor Father Tim when I make my Russian sign of the cross, backward as he sees it. I go home and pray and read. I have one glass vodka."

"Doesn't anyone invite you home for Christmas dinner? Your classmates or the people at the Russian Center?"

"I'm not very close to any of them. It is my fault. All I would have to do is hint."

"*Well,* someone should take you home for dinner on Christmas Day."

Guess who that someone was.

Odessa did not look at me.

Did she expect an invitation to meet my family?

Why wouldn't she?

Even after I told her what a dysfunctional bunch they were?

Did that make any difference?

Well, I wouldn't do it.

"There is a beautiful poem about Christmas," Odessa said. "May I quote it?"

We agreed, not that there was much choice.

> *"Some say, that ever 'gainst that season comes*
> *Wherein our Savior's birth is celebrated,*
> *The bird of dawning singeth all night long:*
> *The nights are wholesome; then no planets strike,*
> *No fairy takes, nor witch has power to charm*
> *So hallow'd and so gracious is the time."*

"What a lovely poem! Is it Russian?"

"Of course," Odessa said, stealing a quick glance at me.

"Yep," I said, "a Russian poet named William Shakespeare."

"Everyone knows he's Russian," she insisted. "Like Dickens and Sir Walter Scott and even William Faulkner."

General laughter.

" 'So gracious is the time,' " she repeated the line. "We should never forget that verse."

All of us agreed.

She slept on the MBTA ride back from Chestnut Hill. Odessa, I had discovered, could sleep on almost any occasion.

A great gift.

I did not propose that she come to Chicago for Christmas. No way.

Did I realize that I would do so eventually?

Maybe I did. But I did not want to think about the confrontation between the loud contentious shanty Irish and my mystical beloved.

Yeah, by then she was beloved.

"Your father is home from Bosnia?" she asked me when we got off the train from Harvard Square.

Not bad for someone who had just awakened.

"I guess so."

"Haven't you called him?"

"I'll do it tomorrow."

"Wouldn't it be better to do it tonight?" she said, gesturing towards the bank of public phones.

So I called. He was home all right, undamaged and raging about the failure of the United States to take on the Serbs.

"You want another Vietnam?"

Silence for a moment.

"I guess not."

"He's home and as feisty as ever," I said to Odessa after we had hung up.

"He was nevertheless happy that you phoned him."

"Not so you'd notice it."

On the Tuesday of the second week in December I brought her the huge collection of oils that I had purchased for her Christmas present.

She didn't do what an American might have done: protest that it was all too much.

Instead she hugged me fervently.

"How wonderfully thoughtful of you, Ivan! You are such a thoughtful person."

"Prince Ivan the Thoughtful."

"Certainly. . . . I will celebrate Christmas all year long with this gift. I will have to redo you in oil and color."

"No rush about that."

"I will try another self-portrait. With my clothes on."

"That would spoil the fun."

She turned crimson again.

"Perhaps."

Then I reached in my book bag and removed the two roundtrip tickets from Boston to Chicago.

"I've made my family seem unappealing, Odessa. To tell you the truth I've understated the case. Brigie is the only one who has any sense. Still I'd like to spend Christmas with you. Maybe you can help me put up with them."

"I can't afford the ticket to Chicago," she said primly.

"This is the second part of your Christmas present."

"It is too much. It is not right."

"It's not too much. It is too right."

"No."

"Look at all the time you spent on my Russian."

"That was fun."

"Well, if you're in Chicago, Christmas will be fun for me."

"Will it *really*?"

"Yes it will *really*."

She paused.

"Thank you very much, Ivan. I would love to spend Christmas with you."

So that was that.

This was the acid test. I couldn't imagine a young woman wanting to marry into my family.

She hugged me and kissed me again.

So easy to make her happy.

Well, it would be an interesting experience.

That night I called home to break the news.

As luck would have it, Dad answered the phone.

"You're bringing a woman home for Christmas?" he exploded. "What is she?"

"Russian," I said.

"A Communist? I won't have one of them in my house."

"She's not a Communist, Dad. Her grandfathers were both priests."

"Not Catholic priests!"

"Russian Orthodox. The Russian Catholics have married priests."

"Not Catholic priests."

"Yes, they do."

"I never heard of anything like that."

"Then you weren't listening in theology classes at Notre Dame."

"Well, you'll have to use separate bedrooms. I won't have unmarried people sleeping together in my house."

"We're not sleeping together, Dad. She can have my room and I'll use the room in the basement."

"Well, I don't know. . . ."

"Tell Mom."

"I don't know. . . ."

"Tell her."

I hung up.

He'd tell her all right. Like everyone else who had met Tatiana, he'd fall in love with her.

I hoped.

CHAPTER

3

"This is the woman who did the sketch of you?"

"Yeah."

Mom had weighed in first thing in the morning.

"She's Russian?"

"Speaks good English."

"I don't care about that. . . . What's her name?"

"She goes by a couple of names. I guess Tatiana Alekseevna will do."

"Are you still not sleeping with her?"

"I'm not a pagan, Mom."

"If you are, we can simply ignore your father."

"No!"

"Okay. . . . Are you in love with her?"

"Hard to tell for sure."

"Can I make an appointment for her with some-one at the Art Institute?"

"I guess so. I'll have to ask her, but I don't think she'll mind."

"I hope Fiona likes her."

I hadn't thought of Fiona. She was a recent ad-dition to the family—a large and affectionate and slobbery Irish Wolfhound.

"She will, Mom. Everyone likes Tatiana."

Mom would, Fiona would, Brigid certainly would. Ed? Maria? Steph? Joe? Dad?

Maybe and maybe not.

The next call was from Little Sister.

"She's really coming to Chicago for Christmas?"

"Unless she changes her mind."

"Her name is Trish?"

"Not exactly. Tatiana."

"Totally cool! Is she completely gorgeous."

I lied.

"She's all right, I guess. High cheekbones and slightly slanted eyes. Looks like an American In-dian."

"Native American," she corrected me.

"Right."

"There's nothing wrong with that."

"You could say that she's sort of exotic looking."

"Bitchin'! I can hardly wait to meet her. . . . Will I like her?"

"Most everyone does."

"Will she like me?"

"Totally."

"You know what, Jack?"

"No, what?"

"You totally have to take her to the Christmas Ball at the club."

"No."

"You should forget that silly golf tournament thing."

"No."

"Everyone knows you won it."

"No."

"Christmas is a time of forgiveness and love."

"No."

"Does she have a dress for it? Is she my size? She could wear my junior Christmas dance dress."

"Too shocking!"

"You're kidding me?"

"Would I do that?"

"You certainly would. . . . She's too good for you. I know that! Anyway, I'll have my dress cleaned, just in case."

All Odessa would need to be convinced that we

Irish Catholic Americans were total pagans would be the Christmas dance at the club.

I delivered a dozen canvases on stretchers to her apartment. She wasn't home but the landlady, of the same ethnic origins as I, was happy to let me put them inside the door.

"Isn't she a grand young woman now?"

"Isn't she?"

"Didn't she tell me that she's dating a nice Irish boy?"

"Irish American."

" 'Tis all the same, isn't it now?"

So Odessa was telling people that she was dating me. Wasn't that a little premature?

I suppose she was telling them that she was going home with me for Christmas. Well, that hadn't happened yet, had it?

On Thursday it was clear and bitter cold. No kids at the bench.

"Isn't it a wonderful day, Ivan?" she asked as I took her mittened hand in mine.

"Real Russian weather."

"Not that cold at all."

"It'll be colder in Chicago."

"I don't care. . . . Will they like me, Ivan?"

"Who?"

"Your family."

"Most of them will. Everyone likes you, Odessa. Maybe not Steph. She hates all women who are prettier than she is."

"I will be very polite and formal."

"That won't do any good. . . . The question is whether you will like them."

"They're your family. Of course I will like them."

"I think you'll like Brigie and Fiona too."

"Who is Fiona?"

"Wolfhound puppy."

"A *Russian* wolfhound!"

"Nope, Irish. She's all right, but she slobbers a lot."

All right, I was presenting a bleak picture of my family. There was, however, no point in trying to pretend that they were a likable bunch.

I never should have invited her.

"Thank you for the canvases, Ivan," she said. "You are a very generous man."

"Prince Ivan the Generous?"

"Perhaps!"

"There's not much room for them in your apartment."

"Isn't my landlady adorable? She is so nice to me."

"She said you were dating an Irish boy."

"She approved of you. Said you were a real charming gentleman."

"Prince Ivan the Charming."

The day finally came for the trip to Chicago, a gray Sunday with snow flurries. I was able to use my advantage card to upgrade us to first class. It would sure beat Aeroflot.

In Chicago, according to CNN, there was already a layer of snow on the ground. The forecast said bitter cold and clear for most of the day, snow flurries at night. It was still better than Moscow.

I wrongly assumed that she'd be traveling light. However, there were presents to be brought to my family, so we checked everything in. She held my hand as we struggled through the mess and confusion at Logan airport.

"Even at Moscow the airport is never this crowded, Ivan."

We were still talking Russian.

"Wait till you see O'Hare."

"No one is smiling, except you."

"Am I smiling?"

"Since you came for me in the taxi."

"Mistake."

"And you are being very amusing."

"Good for me."

"Should they not be smiling? Are they not going home for Christmas? Ought not they be happy?"

"They don't want to be going home for Christmas, Odessa. It's usually a terrible experience. Parents are nervous, kids become difficult because their schedule is messed up, too much food, too much drink, too much resentment and rivalry from the past, hidden agenda, all over the place."

"Really?"

"Really."

"How sad. Should they not celebrate the coming of the Christ Child?"

"Sure we should. It's just too bad that He came at Christmas."

"Oh."

"Christmas should not come during the holidays."

"Oh . . . I don't think I understand. You Americans have so much to be grateful for."

"You're right, Tatiana Alekseevna. You and I should keep that in mind. Or rather, you should keep reminding me."

The grip of her hand on mine tightened.

"Of course, Ivan."

For the first time I permitted myself to attend

to an idea which had been stewing and frothing in my preconscious: Maybe I should have gotten her a ring for Christmas, instead of oils and canvases.

Premature, Jack Flanigan, much too premature.

Yet when you find your one true love, you should go after her, should you not?

How do you know she's your one true love?

I don't.

Besides, you're not ready to share your life with a woman. You're not old enough.

Yeah?

"Are you Russian?" the cabin attendant, patently Boston Irish, asked me as we claimed our seats.

"The young woman is," I responded. "I'm what you think I am, only I'm a good faker."

"He speaks excellent Russian," Odessa assured her.

She held my hand during take-off, declined a drink, and promptly went to sleep. So I had my Bailey's Irish Cream and hers too.

The weather cleared over southern Michigan. I nudged her.

"We're almost there, Odessa."

She woke up instantly.

"Is that the ocean?"

I had given her the window seat so she could see the city as we came in over the lake.

"No, only Lake Michigan. . . . The Michigan-Huron basin is the largest body of freshwater in the world. Big old melted glacier."

We vectored north of the city, back out over the lake and then headed in for O'Hare at a couple of thousand feet.

"Oh!" she said. "How beautiful!"

"It will do."

"What a joy to live in such a lovely city."

"We have our slums too."

"But such beauty! God lurks everywhere in Chicago!"

That's how I wanted her to react, wasn't it?

The only place more crowded than O'Hare the week before Christmas will be the locus for the Last Judgment. Odessa found it exhilarating.

"A beautiful city should have a beautiful airport, should it not?"

"People are not smiling here either."

"You are, Ivan. That is enough for me. Prince Ivan the Smiling."

She drew my arm tighter in hers.

It was unthinkable that anyone in the family

would pick us up. Dad would send a limo for Steph and Joe and the kids but let Jack and his exotic friend shift for themselves.

So we waited a half hour for our luggage and forty-five minutes for a cab. It was bitter, bitter cold.

"This is more like Moscow cold," Odessa said, as she stood shivering next to me.

I put my arm around her. She snuggled close to me.

"Now I feel warmer, especially since you are still smiling."

Why was Ivan the Smiling so happy?

Did he think he was bringing home a conquest? Or was he looking forward to the clash of wills that would begin when Tatiana Alekseevna entered our house?

We finally made it into the neighborhood. It was already dark and the wind was blowing snow back on the freshly plowed streets. Christmas tree lights glowed everywhere.

"It is like a fairyland, Ivan! So many lovely villas and so much bright light!"

"It's not a bad place to grow up," I admitted.

We unpacked the luggage from the cab and toted it up to the house. I rang the door bell several times. No one answered it. Maybe it was broken. Or maybe they were fighting so loudly that no one heard it.

I finally opened it with my own key, lest we freeze to death. We lugged our stuff inside the door. I took off Odessa's shapeless coat. She was wearing the black jeans, the black turtleneck, and the black boots. Her mother's Greek cross pendant hung around her neck. Her braids were piled high on her head.

Totally bitchin', as Brigid would have said.

We walked into the parlor where the whole bloody gang was shouting at the top of their lungs. The conversation stopped.

"Folks, this is Tatiana Alekseevna Shuskulya. Tatiana, this is my family."

"Good afternoon," she said, tilting her head forward. "I am very happy to be able to spend the day of our Savior's birth with you."

Dead silence. I think everyone gulped. Except Stephanie, whose lip curled up in contempt. Maria stared intently, perhaps trying to determine whether her hatred for her husband's father should extend to the extraordinary young woman who had entered the parlor with an appealing mix of shyness and grace.

Fiona broke the ice. She bounded up and slobbered all over me. I was her favorite, probably because I was the only one in the family who had been nice to her when she was a small puppy last spring. Then she decided that since Odessa was with me, it would be proper to slobber over her too. So she put her feet on my beloved's chest and endeavored to kiss her.

"Such a wonderful dog," Odessa said, hugging Fiona.

"Young woman, are you a Communist?"

Trust my jerk of a father to get right down to business.

"I belonged to the young Communists till I was fourteen, doctor. Then on Easter I had a religious experience and realized that Christ was truly risen. Now I am a Russian Orthodox Christian."

Dad grunted, apparently not convinced of the sincerity of her devotion.

"The cults and sects are quite successful these days in Russia, aren't they?" Ed asked.

Ed gets his worldview from National Public Radio.

"There is now religious freedom in my country . . . yes, nice doggy, very nice doggy. . . . Orthodoxy, however, is not in jeopardy."

Only Brigie got around to hugging our guest.

"Maybe I could make some tea," Mom suggested.

"Perhaps, Ivan," Odessa said to me in Russian, "I might make it now?"

"Sure . . . Mom, Tatiana Alekseevna has brought a Christmas present for the family. She would like to make tea for you, Russian style."

"That would be sweet," Mom said, notably unconvinced.

"Ivan, would you help me arrange matters?"

"That's what I'm here for."

Four little kids who had been engaged in mayhem in the back of the Georgian house appeared in the parlor, two boys and two girls, one of each with red hair. Uncle Joe (Daddy to two of them) was trailing with a storybook in one hand and a broken toy truck in the other. The kids went crazy at the sight of Uncle Jack and hugged him. Then they stared with bold curiosity at the exotic young woman who was unpacking a samovar, Russian tea glasses, and a couple of packages of Russian cookies.

Odessa's act was the one I'd seen before, but this time it was more elaborate.

"In Russia we see that tea is a great gift from

God. On cold winter days like this one, families gather around the samovar and drink tea together. It warms their bodies and their souls. However, we must prepare it properly, with respect and gratitude. Even the poorest people in Russia who have very little in life, still have their family samovar and their tea. Even if they don't have cookies like these."

"Can I have a cookie?" Ed's older son—called Mario despite his red hair—demanded.

"After tea is made and if your mother permits."

It was a good show. No, it was a great show. Everyone watched in fascination. First set to Odessa.

"So, it is now finished." She poured tea in one of the glasses which they call a *stakan* in a holder contraption called a *podstakanchik* ("the little thing under the glass") that the Russians use.

"Missus?" She offered the tea and a small plate of cookies to Mom with a respectful bow.

"Doctor?"

"Uh, yes, sure. Why not?"

She delivered the tea and cookies around the room with total solemnity, in the order of proper seniority, except I was left to the end, even after Brigie.

"Thank you, Ivan."

"Why do you call Uncle Jack Ivan, Tati?" Mario demanded.

"It is his name in Russian. We usually talk in Russian."

"Ivan the Terrible?" Eddie sneered.

"Ivan the Wonderful," she replied serenely, forcing my brother back into his hole in the woodwork.

"Bitchin'," Brigie whispered in my ear. "And we're the same size. She *could* wear my dress from last year."

"Too much cleavage," I whispered back.

"Damn good tea," Dad announced. "Good cookies, too. Tea is good for you, you know."

"Of course," Odessa agreed.

Did she know what she was doing? Did she realize that she had rocked my obnoxious, contentious family back on their heels? Was it all a planned routine?

So what if it was?

"Are these homemade cookies, dear?" Mom asked.

"Of course."

"You made them?"

"Yes."

"They are very, very good."

"Thank you, missus."

"Can we have cookies, Tati?" Mario demanded.

Odessa glanced at Maria.

"Only one," Maria said.

"They are very small, missus," she said, tentatively lifting a second finger.

Maria's brilliant smile appeared, which it rarely did in our family circle. She nodded conspiratorially.

"Do you tell stories?" Gena, Steph's fragile daughter, also a redhead, asked shyly.

"Of course I tell stories."

"Would you tell us a story, *please*, Aunt Tati?"

"May I?" Odessa glanced around the room.

No one said she could not, so she was off and running. "Ivan, will you give me my sketch pad? I will illustrate the story."

"Yes, your highness?"

"Your *highness*?" Steph exploded.

"Certainly," I replied. "Tatiana Alekseevna is a grand duchess in disguise."

"She certainly looks like one. Totally!" Brigid announced.

Odessa blushed but, sitting cross-legged on the floor, began the story, illustrating it with rapid sketches as she talked. It featured the usual run of characters—Vasilisa the Wise, Baba Yaga, Prince Ivan the Wonderful, the wicked king—but there were some newcomers, the Snow Maiden, Grandfather Frost ("Who is just like Santa Claus"), and the Christmas Angel. The wicked king wanted to chop down all the Christmas trees, but Vasilisa and Baba Yaga and the Snow Maiden and Grandfather Frost wouldn't let him. Even Prince Ivan made a minor contribution to the happy ending, when Christmas presents were passed out to all the children in Russia.

The kids laughed and jumped and shouted and crowded around to see the drawings. So did Joe Devine, Maria, and Mom. Everyone else listened. Except Joe who was scribbling rapidly, doubtless taking notes for one of his classes.

Second set to Tatiana Alekseevna, or Aunt Tati as she was now being called.

That was kind of premature, wasn't it?

"Aunt Tati, who is the Snow Maiden?"

"Well once upon a time, long, long ago, in a small town in Russia, there was a good and virtuous couple who could not have children, no matter how hard they tried. One cold winter day, they decided to make a snowman. Only as they worked on him, he became a snowwoman and then a snow little girl. They made a beautiful cloak for her with a wonderful fur neck ruff. Before long the snow maiden's eyes began to flicker and then her cheeks turned a lovely color. Then there stood before them this gorgeous little girl with deep blue eyes and long blond hair. 'Who are you?' they asked.

" 'I have come to you from the land of ice and snow. I am your own little girl.'

"So she became their little girl and played with all the children in the village and everyone loved her. But when the snow began to melt, she turned listless and unhappy. Finally she came to them and sang a little song:

" *The time has come for me to go*
'Away up North to the land of snow.'

"Her mother held her in her arms so she couldn't leave, but soon all the mother had in her arms was cold water. The snow maiden could not live in springtime."

"Oh, Aunt Tati," one of the little girls cried. "How terrible!"

"Shh! I'm not finished. The next year when it

was icy cold outside, her parents heard a loud knock at the door. They couldn't imagine who it would be on such a bitter night. But the stranger kept knocking. Finally they opened the door and it was . . ."

"The Snow Maiden!"

"Right! And she sang them a little song:

> " *'Mother, Father, let me in!*
> *'The snow has brought me back again!'*

"And she spent every winter with them and they all lived happily ever after. And every year at *Sviatki*—Christmastime—Russians tell the story of the Snow Maiden, *Snegurochka*, to show that love is as strong as death!"

Applause!

"A Russian composer even wrote an opera about her," I said.

I was ignored. As I deserved to be.

"Can you do the dance, Aunt Tati?" Brigid asked.

"The dance?"

"You know, the one where you fold your arms and kick."

"The *Kazatska?* The Cossack dance?"

"I bet that's it."

"Every Russian man can do the *Kazatska*," Odessa replied firmly. "Some women do it, though traditionally they are not supposed to. I have done it. Often. Though not recently."

She glanced at me for my verdict.

"Why not?" I said in Russian.

"I may make a fool of myself."

"They'll love you all the more."

"I need a bare wooden floor," she said in English.

"Our morning room has a wooden floor, dear," Mom was watching my grand duchess closely—and approvingly.

As well she might.

No cross-exam even.

"Is your family in Russia, dear?"

Okay, the cross-exam was beginning.

We all moved into the morning room, Stephanie reluctantly and with much facial protest. I cleared away some of the more readily destructible furniture.

"I have no family, missus. Both of my parents are with God."

She turned to me, "Ivan, you do know the music?"

"Certainly."

"Good. I now need one glass vodka."

"Of course."

Our vodka bottle wasn't in the fridge and hence not cold like it should be.

I filled a tumbler to the top.

"Thank you, Ivan," she bowed to me.

"It's kind of warm."

She lifted her shoulder in a familiar shrug.

"That's a lot of booze, young woman," my father warned ominously.

She pondered the one glass vodka.

"Only one glass, doctor. I never take a second. No Russian can do the Cossack dance without one glass vodka. No one dares to do it with more than one."

A bit of an exaggeration, but it shut the old fella up.

She downed the vodka the Russian way, in a single gulp. A few of us shuddered.

"Now Prince Ivan knows the music. He will sing it for you once. You must clap your hands when he claps them. I hope God protects me from making a complete fool of myself."

So I went through the music, clapping at the appropriate places. Everyone, except Steph, joined in. Fiona barked but somewhat out of the appropriate rhythm. Odessa was bouncing up and down on her feet, getting in the mood for the *Kazatska*, surely the silliest dance humankind has ever invented.

"Be careful," I said to her in Russian.

She dismissed me with a wave of her hand.

"Now we begin."

I took for granted that, graceful woman that she was, she would do the dance gracefully. I was surprised that she threw herself into it with abandoned vigor. She kicked and shouted and squatted and hollered and laughed—all with total defiance. The audience whipped itself into a frenzy, caught in the mania and abandon of this astonishing young woman.

It was a show and a half.

Her face turned red, her breathing grew more rapid, her steps slowed down.

Time to stop, I thought.

She waited too long.

One of her feet slipped out from under her, she tried to regain her balance, missed a step, and then fell unceremoniously to the floor. Then my nonlaughing grand duchess collapsed into a fit of wild laughter.

Fiona, thinking perhaps she was a St. Bernard, leaped over a couple of chairs, dashed to the fallen dancer, and began licking her face.

Odessa laughed all the harder. The kids ran to embrace her and laughed with her, figuring that's what they were supposed to do.

Everyone in the room was laughing, myself included, ungallant man that I was.

Well, Dad wasn't laughing.

"Did you hurt yourself, young woman?"

"Thank you doctor, but I will not require surgery."

Brigid finally helped her up off the floor.

"Nor, missus, will I sue!"

The assembly applauded loudly.

Fiona barked.

Odessa bowed solemnly.

"Perhaps I should have practiced."

More applause.

"Ivan, may I please have another cup of tea?"

"With ice cubes in it?"

"Do not be blasphemous!"

Men and women shook hands with her or hugged her. Even Stephanie told her that it was "super."

Mom offered to show her up to her room.

I carried her bags up the stairs, deposited them in her room, which had once been my room, and discreetly departed.

Mom was continuing the cross-examination as I went down the stairs.

"Do you plan to go back to Russia, my dear?"

She got the same answer as I did:

"Perhaps."

On the first floor, the women of the family were setting the table for dinner.

"She's incredible, Jack," Maria said with a wide smile. "Astonishing!"

"She's all right."

"You, simply like totally, have got to take her to the Christmas dance, Jack," Brigie added.

"At the country club?" Maria looked up at me. "I hate that place more than you do, Jack, but if Tatiana will be there, I'll go too, won't we, Ed?"

"Certainly. She's a kind of stereotype, isn't she Jack, but a charming stereotype."

"I've been to the country three times," I replied. "There's no one there quite like her."

I carried my meager luggage to my windowless room in the basement. The room was cold, forty degrees according to the thermostat. Naturally no one had thought to turn up the heat. I pushed the arrow to eighty and sat on the edge of the bed to organize my thoughts.

I could not have anticipated the magnitude of her triumph. She had dazzled them on first contact. What would happen next?

At supper she had shed her black jeans and sweater for the charcoal turtleneck dress, removed her jewelry, and lowered her hair.

"Are you all right?" I asked her in Russian.

"A few aches, but I am fine. I will sleep well tonight."

"You really are a crazy Russian, aren't you, Tatiana Alekseevna?"

"Of course."

She declined wine with the dinner. "Not after one glass vodka."

"Are you a Cossack, Aunt Tati?" Steph asked her.

The kids, by the way, were all sound asleep.

"Oh, no. I am mostly Great Russian. I have some Ukrainian blood too. And there must be a touch of Tartar on my mother's side because I have such high cheekbones and my eyes slant a little."

"It's a very attractive mix, my dear," Mom insisted.

"Thank you, missus."

"You could not celebrate Christmas under Socialism, could you?" Ed asked, always in search of the inside story.

"It varied. Sometimes only in secret. My grandfather, before they sent him to the labor camp where he died, would come over to our house and offer Divine Worship. The Party transferred a lot of Christmas customs to New Year's Day. Those of us who believed always pretended that they were Christmas customs anyway. Now we can do what we want and many of us are returning to the old Russian ways again. They can be very serious ways."

"How so?" Joe Devine wondered. He was drinking in the whole show, preparing for the story he would tell his class after the first of the year. "They still tell stories, don't they?"

Joe, it dawned on me, was not an actor or a writer. He was a *seanachie*, an ancient and honorable Irish profession. It enjoyed higher status than any other in our ancestral society.

"We would not be Russians without stories, Mr. Joseph. We even tell long stories about our fasting, some of them even true. We fast for the month before, very serious fast. This will be the first Christmas since I have been in America I have not fasted. Still, missus, I hope you don't mind, I will fast on the eve of our Lord's birth. Only a piece of bread and a cup of tea."

"My name is Annie, dear."

"Yes, missus. I will fast until the first star appears that evening. It will call to mind both the star that led the Magi and Jesus who is the light of the world. The day before Christmas is also a day for the fast of our souls, we give up all bad thoughts and speech, all anger and conflict, and wait in composure for the Savior that is coming to us. Darkness falls and we continue to wait. Then the first star appears. It marks the beginning of a new day and of the glorious feast of our Lord's birth. With the rising of that star we permit the light of the Lord to begin to shine on us. We think of the words from St. Peter's epistle, 'You will do well to take heed of the light shining in the darkness, until the day dawn and the daystar arise in your hearts.'"

Again everyone was silent, not so much embarrassed by Odessa's piety as awed by it.

"That's very beautiful, child," the old fella said. "Perhaps we American Catholics could learn much from you."

I never thought I would hear him say such words to anyone. Ever.

"It is a very holy time of the year. We should try to be holy in our hearts, though it be very difficult. Easter is a holier time, but Christmas is holy too."

"I'm afraid we don't have much time for holiness," Mom said with a sigh.

"How many people keep those customs now?" Ed asked.

"Not everyone, of course. Many do not, but even in Moscow many do. For seventy-five years there was no religion. It is astonishing that so many have returned to it so quickly. I think perhaps we even surprise ourselves."

"With all the travel, especially with children," Joe Devine made one of his rare contributions to the discussion.

"We must struggle with it," Odessa agreed, "but was not the great Russian poet right when he said:

"Some say, that ever 'gainst that season comes
Wherein our Savior birth is celebrated,
The bird of dawning singeth all night long:
The nights are wholesome; then no planets strike,

*No fairy takes, nor witch has power to charm
So hallow'd and so gracious is the time."*

Joe was grinning already, a storyteller relishing another storyteller's trick.

"Did a Russian write that?" Brigie said with a frown.

"Of course, Miss Brigid, a Russian named William Shakespeare."

More laughter.

She had made her point, however, and had cast her magic spell on all of us. For our family it was a pleasant Sunday-before-Christmas dinner.

I was proud of her, with no reason to justify my pride because I had nothing to do with her being magic.

"I may make some Russian Christmas bread on the eve of the feast, mis—I mean, Annie?"

"You can make anything you want, dear."

Odessa devoured two dishes of ice cream.

"Russians are addicted to ice cream," she explained. "And, doctor, it is much less harmful than vodka."

"So long as you exercise, child, which I'm sure you do."

"Already I have agreed to run with Miss Brigid in the morning."

"It is very cold."

"You have never been in Moscow in December."

The bird of Christmas was singing loudly and the daystar was glowing in the sky. Anything might happen.

It was also agreed that in the morning Mom would take her down to the Art Institute and deliver her to the yacht club for lunch with me. I would then take her to the Russian Liturgical Art exhibit at the Field Museum and finally out to the university for an appointment with a man in the art history program.

"I hope I have not embarrassed you too much, Ivan?" she said as I escorted her to her room after supper.

"Do I look embarrassed?"

"No, you look very happy. . . . Yes, doggie, you may certainly sleep in my room tonight. . . . You are not too uncomfortable in the basement?"

"I'm fine. . . . You were great, Odessa, sensational. They love you."

"I'm glad you are pleased, Ivan the Wonderful."

It occurred to me that she was expecting a kiss.

So I kissed her, very quietly because of the circumstances.

She seemed satisfied.

Ed and Maria, who lived only a block away, had gone home with their sleeping kids. Steph and Joe were staying with us. Together with Mom and Dad they were in the parlor watching the ten o'clock news.

"Would everyone please note," I said loudly, "that I am returning to my virtuous monastic cell in the basement?"

"That's nice, dear," Mom murmured, not having heard a word of what I had said.

"Grand."

"Storytellers are wonderful, aren't they, Joe?" Steph said softly. "I never realized before just how wonderful."

The temperature in said cell had risen to a pleasant seventy-five. I did not turn it down.

Though I was keyed up from the excitement of the day, I floated easily into sleep.

I was not unaware of the meaning behind Odessa's conquest of my family. They all had made up their minds that I should marry my grand duchess. At that point, it didn't seem such a bad idea.

She had transformed them all. It would not be permanent. It might not even last till the next day. But if we could sustain a bit of it through Christmas, perhaps some of them would have an opportunity to grow a little bit and change somewhat.

The name of such a possibility, I think, is grace. Maybe even Grace.

That's what you expect from a graceful grand duchess.

CHAPTER

4

I stumbled upstairs for breakfast about eight thirty to a babble of women's voices: my two sisters and Odessa in running clothes and as thick as the proverbial thieves, drinking coffee around the kitchen table.

"We went running, Ivan," Odessa informed me.

"Patently."

They were covered with sweat and the zippers on their jackets were open and disclosed running bras which in the strange world of women's lingerie did not constitute lingerie and hence could be displayed without immodesty.

"We went to church too," Brigid added.

"Father was quite surprised at Tati's Russian

sign of the cross," Stephanie concluded. "But he smiled."

"He would."

"Fiona doggie came with us," Odessa said. "She was very good in church. She also slept in my bed last night."

"Less demanding than a man."

"About that I would not know."

Laughter.

"What is that painting you're hiding from me?"

"This painting? Oh, it is merely what I will take to the Institute with missus this morning."

"It's never called the Institute, Odessa. Always the Art Institute. . . . Let me see it!"

I poured myself some of their coffee.

"No!" they replied with a common giggle.

I knew who the subject was.

"You will not like it," Odessa said sadly, as she turned it so I could see it.

It was an oil version of the Ivan sketch. She had skewered me perfectly.

"Nice," I admitted grudgingly. "Very nice."

"I think it is very attractive," Steph observed.

"A work of love," Brigie agreed.

"I wouldn't buy a used car from him."

At that point Doctor arrived in a brown sports

coat and matching slacks, the tall, slender surgeon at the beginning of his solemn high procession to the hospital. His silver hair was combed perfectly, his handsome face cleanly shaven, his cologne filling the room, his glasses burnished to a shine. Doctor permitted himself a half cup of coffee, no more. He never sat at the table to drink it. Rather he consumed it as the procession continued to his Cadillac in the garage. The cup was left on a shelf in the garage so he could retrieve it on his return. Doctor rarely spoke to anyone during this ritual.

"Did you do that, young woman? My wife will have to be the one to judge its artistic merits. Nonetheless you have captured my second son perfectly."

Three sentences. Major departure from normal.

"Second son from the second city," I observed.

Doctor was already gone.

"Did he like it?" Odessa asked softly.

His three children assured her that what the doctor had said was high praise indeed.

I would call Lincoln Park Zoo to determine whether the other leopards were changing their spots.

"Tomorrow Maria will run with us too," Odessa informed me.

"Of course."

Mom dropped Odessa off at the Chicago Yacht Club precisely at noon. She was wearing a dark brown sweater and a long matching skirt—artist on a cold day. Artist with gorgeous breasts on a cold day. She slumped against me as I kissed her. So I repeated the kiss.

"Bad morning?" I said as I hung her shabby coat in the cloak room.

"As you know, Ivan," she replied in Russian, "I love neatness and order in my life. Now I am disconcerted. I have no plan."

"They liked you at the Art Institute?"

"They liked my work," she corrected me. "I do not know what to do. You must kiss me again, Ivan. Please."

My third effort was lingering and reassuring.

"Thank you."

"You must make all your decisions instantly, immediately, before lunch is over."

"You know me too well. . . . My what a beautiful place. . . . There are boats here in the summer?"

"Tons of them."

Mr. Foster showed us to our table.

"You are a very attractive man, Ivan."

What was that leading up to?

"Thank you."

"I have been able to find only one serious fault in you."

"Gotta look harder."

"You sulk."

"Tell me about it."

"It is absurd to hate Harvard after all these years. They made a foolish mistake. It is their loss, not yours."

"I don't hate some people from Harvard."

"I have noticed that. . . . Now tell me about the fight with the club."

I should have seen it coming.

"You want to go to the Christmas dance?"

"That does not matter to me, though your sisters want me to go."

"Brigid's dress fits you?"

"Adequately," she said with a blush. "It is the most immoral dress I have ever thought of wearing."

"I can hardly wait. . . . We'll go to the dance, Odessa. The women in my life outnumber me."

"That is not the point, Ivan, and you know it."

Come to think of it, she would make an excellent, if stern, mother abbess.

"The point is," I said, giving up the fight, "that I shouldn't sulk."

"Yes. . . . Tell me the story."

"Will you give me absolution if I do?"

"Perhaps."

I waited till our soup was served and tried to explain to someone who had never seen a golf match what the championship round in September was like.

I can't hit a wood to save my life. Two hundred yards with the wind behind me is absolute max. But I'm pretty good with the irons, especially the short irons and the putter. The doctor drafted me for the tournament while I was still in Russia. I played only one practice round. I was five strokes off the lead going into Sunday. Most of the club had dismissed me as a young punk, arguably a young Communist punk, who was not a serious golfer.

The temperature plummeted twenty degrees on Saturday night and a cold, mean rain greeted us when we teed off. I was still on jet lag, cold, wet, discouraged, and didn't give a damn. So I played the best golf of my life. All the circuits in my head clicked, and I went with the flow. Tied the course record. Ten under par. Four birds and three eagles, two of the latter on the last two holes—an ace on seventeen and a chip in on eighteen. The reaction of the membership was underwhelming.

That Flanigan punk couldn't possibly have won. I took the two trophies home regardless, the traveling trophy and the one I could keep permanently. The fogies at the club were outraged. The club's reputation would suffer. Not only couldn't I have won, I didn't win. I had cheated. Never mind that the second-and third-place players had been in the foursome with me and reported that my four-stroke victory was honest. Three of the fogies went to the board on Monday to launch a protest and demand that I be disqualified.

I was so furious that I drove over to the club that afternoon, threw the trophies on the lobby floor, and stalked out like I was Finn MacCool. The next day I stormed off to B.C., swearing to all who would listen that I would never set foot in that (deleted) club again.

"Bravo, Ivan!" the grand duchess said.

Mom figured there was no point in being a litigator unless you could take care of your own. She wrote tough letters to the three fogies accusing them of defamation. She demanded a written apology and a retraction of the charges. They tried to laugh her off. Then their own lawyers warned them of the dangers of trying to take on

Annie Mahoney and they backed down. I received copies of the three letters of apology and a letter from the board. I tore them up. End of story.

"Ivan," she said in mild reproof.

"Yes?"

"Would it not have been nice to accept the apology and forget the whole incident?"

"Harumpf," I grumbled.

"It doesn't really make you feel good, does it?"

"Actually it does."

"No it doesn't. You're bigger than they are. This is Christmas, the time that God discloses his forgiving love to all of us."

"Harumpf," I grumbled again, but this time with a grin.

Then I said something which I would never have dreamed of saying before I had stumbled upon my Odessa.

"You're right."

I must truly be falling in love. No, in love.

"Really?" she seemed astonished.

"We will go to the dance. I will be charming and loving and forgiving."

And take great pride in showing off my glorious date in the immoral dress.

I didn't say that.

"I hope you will never sulk at me, Ivan," she said, lowering her eyes.

I touched her fingers.

"Not a chance."

In the dark and gloomy basement of the Field Museum, we entered the magical world of Russian religious art—icons and veils and vestments and chalices. Most of the work was from Alaska and the Aleutians and from North America, but it was still in the center of the Russian tradition. The recorded choir of St. Tikhon seminary sang in the background. I discovered there were a number of Russian saints from North America, most notably St. Herman of Kodiak, St. Innocent of Sitka, and St. Tikhon of North America himself.

Odessa held my hand and wept softly as we walked through the exhibition.

"It is so beautiful, Ivan. Like I was home."

"What a shame our two heritages are separated. The Pope could end it tomorrow if he climbed down a little off his high horse."

"I don't think so. Our distrust of you is very strong. And it is all so foolish. On both sides."

"A thousand years of history."

"Still foolish," she insisted. "One God, one Savior, one God-Bearer."

She squeezed my hand very hard, perhaps to say that the foolishness wouldn't stand in our way. In that dark room with the glorious icons all around us and the wondrous music in the background, I was not of a mind to disagree.

The professor at the university kept us waiting for half an hour. Then he explained that their program was very small, they took few students, and only the best, perhaps Tatiana should apply to Indiana University or even University of Illinois at Chicago. He rose to dismiss us.

She handed him her transcript.

He glanced quickly at it.

"Interesting," he mumbled.

She gave him a sealed letter from one of her professors.

He opened it, scanned it briefly.

"Very interesting."

"This is one of my papers."

He read the first page and put the paper aside.

"I will read this with great interest tonight."

"Thank you."

"Well, you should definitely apply here. I'll talk

to my colleagues and see if we can work something out."

We took our leave.

"Thank you, Ivan," Odessa said as we emerged from the dark building to the snow covered and glistening Midway.

"I didn't get angry."

"You did too, and you had reason to be angry, but . . ."

"I didn't sulk."

"That's right," she said, kissing me.

It was okay for my Russian witch to reform, however temporarily, the rest of my family. But she had no right to reform me, did she?

On Christmas Eve, Mom and Maria joined in the morning run. Doctor actually smiled at Odessa and said, "Good morning, young woman."

Then Aunt Tati set about making a *matrioshka* doll for our Christmas tree. A *matrioshka* is one of those collections of delicately painted wooden dolls, one inside of another. In the absence of the real thing, she made an equivalent one out of paper and crayons, with each doll presenting the face of someone in the family. The kids, who had materialized near her, watched with fascination.

First there was "doctor," the biggest of the dolls,

then "Mama Annie," then Ed and Maria, next a doll with both their children's faces, then Joe and Steph followed by their kids. The next doll was a funny-looking guy with red hair and a green windbreaker. The kids howled at that one. Then a lovely young woman with red hair. Finally at the end there appeared a dizzy-looking large canine head with a red and green ribbon round its neck. She wasn't slobbering.

The sketches were drawn hastily with a minimum of lines. They were, however, mercilessly accurate. Or so I thought when I saw the goof with the red hair.

Then she attached a jingle bell to the bottom and led the kids (and "Fiona doggie") in solemn procession to the tree where, with much ceremony and a prayer that God protect everyone in the *matrioshka*, the dolls were affixed to the tree.

Joe drew a picture of a baby, gave it to Odessa, who added it to their branch of the tree.

"That's my little brother," his son announced.

"No, my little sister," his sister argued.

Stephanie was crying. She gathered her two children into her arms.

This was going a little too far, too fast, wasn't it?

I thought the branch bent a little.

Odessa told more stories to the kids and spent much of the day in the kitchen, making bread and cakes and cookies (one of which, but only one, she put in my mouth like it was Holy Communion) and singing Russian Christmas carols.

I was dispatched to buy caviar ("the very best you can find"), raspberries, cranberries, sour cream, and buckwheat flour. "Also one bottle very good rum."

I obediently did what I was told.

Upon return I heard women singing in the kitchen—*kolyada*, Russian Christmas carols—and laughing as they sang.

In the kitchen all the women of the family, Mom, Steph, Maria, Brigid, and Odessa, were red-faced from laughter and song.

"Aunt Tati is teaching us Russian carols," Mom explained.

"Ah," I said. Perhaps she was a witch.

"This one you can translate as follows," she said, ignoring me.

> *"Let us thank thee, God in the heavens.*
> *Let us praise thee,*
> *Let us worship our lord*

of the earth,
Let us worship him!
May his good servants never grow old!
Let us worship him!
Let us sing praises for Our Lord!
Let us sing praises for Him!
Praise God, Praise! Praise Him!
Praise God, Praise! Praise Him!"

"It sounds better in Russian," she informed us. "Ivan, you have brought the fruit and the rum and the caviar?"

"Best money can buy."

"I will make *rom-baba* and *kissel* and *blini.* But you must not eat any of it now."

The other women, having bonded with Odessa and thus with one another, laughed at her warning.

I took the hint and left the kitchen. They continued to laugh at me. Better that I stay out of everyone's way till mass time, especially Aunt Tati.

Blini, by the way, is a very thin pancake filled with caviar and covered with sour cream, *Kissel* is a delectable fruit custard. *Rom-baba* is a sponge cake liberally doused with rum and round in shape, like a woman is. I can't help it if that's a sexist name. Am I Russian?

All three are delicious. Brigie would tell us on Christmas Day that we must have them every Christmas.

Hint, hint.

I would ignore it.

The young parents and their children would attend the five o'clock children's mass. Mom, Dad, Brigie, and I would show up for the traditional midnight mass. Odessa of course wanted to go to both of them.

"We must celebrate the Lord's birth with all our fellow Christians," she insisted.

"Did you know, Jack," Brigie asked me breathlessly, "that in Russia they used to believe that, if a young woman looked in a mirror at the very second of midnight, she'd see the face of the man she would some day marry?"

"Too bad that you and that superstitious Russian woman will be in church precisely at midnight."

I tagged along with Odessa to the children's mass. She loved it. Her face shone with an ethereal glow and her lips parted in a glorious smile.

"Is it not wonderful, Ivan? So many little children see the Christ Child as one of them?"

"They make a lot of noise and they want their presents."

"You don't mean that. You adore children. Your nieces and nephews know that. So they swarm all over you."

So there.

At our traditional stand-up buffet after the kids' mass, Odessa, permitting herself one bite of a roll, dropped another bomb.

"In my country husbands and wives say their best lovemaking comes on this holy night. They give themselves to each other with abandon in imitation of Jesus who empties himself totally for humankind, even though he was God, becoming like us in all things, save sin alone."

"The Church approves of this?" Ed asked.

"The Church says nothing. Even the priests are married. How could the Church criticize the fullness of human love?"

"You think men and women should be abandoned in their lovemaking?" Steph inquired.

"What do I know about it? I know only what married people whisper to me. They say that the more abandoned their love, the better it is and the more it reflects God's love."

"I think it is a beautiful custom, Aunt Tati," Maria said. "We Americans are too inhibited."

Now Odessa threw the game-winner.

"It was said by the very old peasants in my country—and now it is said again—that on some very special Christmas nights Mary and Joseph and the Child come back to earth. There is snow on the ground and the nights are cold but not too cold. The blanket of stars in the sky is like a blanket of spring flowers. The angels and the shepherds and the shepherds' children and the twelve wise men come with them."

"Twelve?" Dad asked. "I thought there were only three."

"We Russians know better. . . . It is also said that when men and women of faith who know where the cave is enter it to gaze on the Child, they see something truly amazing."

"What's that?"

"They see that the face of the Child is their own face. Then they realize they are the beloved Child! Is that not wondrous!"

"It's our birthday too," Joe Devine exclaimed. "How wonderful!"

I had never heard of the lovemaking custom before. I wasn't sure that it existed. Odessa, however, had her own game plan. Who was I to question it? Her narrative had certainly turned my family to a quiet and expectant lot. A night of love might make for a mellow Christmas.

We walked over to the parish for midnight mass, our feet crunching on the snow as the chimes rang out Christmas music. Above us the stars seemed to look down with complacent joy. They had seen many Christmases. Each one was different.

"You know what, Tatiana Alekseevna?"

"What, Ivan Eduardovich?"

"I don't have a wife with whom to make abandoned love tonight."

"I am aware of that."

"I guess I'm going to have to settle for one passionate kiss."

"I will await it with interest."

The splendor of the midnight mass—music, light, flowers, the joy of saying Merry Christmas—overwhelmed her. She wept throughout the ceremony. Russians weep the most when they're happy.

"It is unbearably beautiful," she said to me. "We can learn much from you Catholics."

"We should incorporate your custom about Christmas love."

"Of course."

After mass we wished Mom and Dad Merry Christmas. Odessa hugged and kissed both of them. She and I walked home with our arms around each other's shoulders, Prince Ivan the Nice if Useless and a combination of Vasilisa the Wise, the Snow Maiden, and Baba Yaga.

Odessa had reason to be happy. She had lost her parents. Now there were other parents, a little odd perhaps, but fond of her. She had perhaps always wanted a sister. Now she had three of them, all of whom adored her. I assumed she had wished for a faithful Russian wolfhound. Now she had a faithful wolfhound, admittedly of a somewhat different ethnic background. She had certainly wondered what it would be like to have a young man. Now she had one, though his qualifications were inadequate. He would do until someone better came along. If he were smart and clever and resourceful—none of which I was—he might be able to fend off better qualified rivals.

Presumably she also wanted a congregation to whom she could preach. She certainly had that.

Best Christmas ever for Odessa?

Best Christmas in America anyway.

We beat Mom and Dad home. Nice doggie

Fiona greeted us enthusiastically. Steph and Joe were in bed. Were they experimenting with Christmas abandon?

Certainly.

I escorted Odessa and Fiona to their room. At the door, I took her in my arms. She submitted eagerly. Our kiss was wildly and forcefully passionate. She surrendered to the demands of my lips and then responded with her own demands.

First one like that for either of us.

"Oh, Ivan," she sighed. "That was wonderful. Christmas love."

"Right."

I kissed her forehead, released her, and prepared to beat a retreat to my monastic cell while I still could.

"I love you, Ivan," she said from the doorway as the slobbering Fiona doggie watched us.

"I love you too, Odessa," I replied lamely. "I always will."

As I went down the stairs to my monastic cell, I did not even regret the implicit promise I had made.

I'd buy her a ring as soon as we returned to Boston. Ask Megan to help me pick it out.

CHAPTER

5

Christmas morning was indeed mellow. Even the kids tore the wrappings off their presents more quietly than kids usually do. The adults, in night dress and robes, were dreamy and content. Brigie raised an eye at me. I shook my head in the negative. She nodded her approval.

Odessa continued to run the show. She told stories to the kids, sang Russian Christmas carols and taught us the choruses to sing with her, and recited poetry.

She began with Pasternak's "Christmas Star" in *Doctor Zhivago.*

"I recite first lines in Russian because it sounds

so beautiful. Then the rest in English so I won't bore you:

> *"Stoyala zima*
> *Dul Yrter iz stepi*
> *I kholodono bylo mladentsu vertepe*
> *na sklone kholma.*

"That means:

> *"It was wintertime*
> *The wind blew from the plain*
> *And the infant was cold*
> *In the cave on the slope of the knoll."*

"Can you recite it all, Aunt Tati?" Maria asked.

"Of course. Every Russian can."

She went through the whole marvelous ode in English and concluded in solemn triumph as the wise men entered:

> *"They spoke in whispers, groping for words*
> *Suddenly one, in deeper shadow, touched another,*
> *To move him aside from the manger, a little to the left.*
> *The other turned, like a guest about to enter,*
> *The star of the nativity was gazing on the maid."*

Sentimental Micks that we were, we all wept as we applauded.

Odessa bowed solemnly in response.

The little brat is having the time of her life, I thought as I applauded more loudly than anyone else.

Russians love to recite poetry, drunk or sober.

They're a word-intoxicated people. My beloved was very good at it, but then she would be.

"May I recite just one more? It is very short?"

Who would dare say no?

"Our Lord comes to everyone with the star
Even those who do not know him
Or have faded him into near forgotten memories
Locked in dark caves of deep regret.
He offers to all what they need most
So that they will be truly happy for many months
And wait passionately for his next return.
On this bright morn, may the daystar remind us
To look under the tree for the special gift
From the one who came to us this day."

More tears, more applause.

"Who wrote that, dear?" Mom asked, totally clueless.

"Tatiana Alekseevna wrote it herself, Mom. Especially for us."

Yet more applause.

Then we opened gifts. I received hairbrushes again, for the third or fourth time.

Shyly Odessa passed out drawings to everyone, The Snow Maiden and Grandfather Frost and the rest of the crowd to the kids who clutched them like they were buried treasure, of the children to their parents, of Brigid and me to my parents, and of Brigid to me.

They were very well done. She must have stayed up half the night working on them.

Everyone proclaimed how wonderful the drawings were.

We dressed for the day, walked in the snow, sang carols for our astonished neighbors, ate Christmas food, especially Russian Christmas pastry and Irish soda bread, and sang songs, listened to stories, ate more food, and drank eggnog, and finally polished off yet another Christmas dinner with still more Russian delicacies.

After dinner Odessa was even persuaded, against all sanity, to attempt the Cossack dance again. This time, in the ultimate insanity, I joined her. No one got hurt.

Then the two of us went for a walk in the quiet, star-illumined night, arms around each other's waists.

"I am very happy, Ivan," she whispered to me. "You were so good to invite me to spend this great feast in your home and with your family."

"It was God's idea," I said, surprisingly myself.

"I know that, but you cooperated with God."

So there, Jack Flanigan.

The celebration ended early. We were all tired, getting irritable, and did not want to ruin the mellowness of the day.

I accompanied Odessa and good dog Fiona to their room and kissed her goodnight, much more modestly than I had in the morning.

"I have a special present for you, Ivan," she whispered. "I did not want to give it to you when the others were there."

She handed me a package in Christmas wrap.

"Thank you," I said.

"Don't open it till you get to your room."

"No, ma'am."

In my cell, I opened it with trembling fingers.

It was what I thought it was, a nude self-portrait. The figure was discreetly covered in gauze, making it even more modest than the first effort. Yet the effect was more erotic as far as I was concerned.

The most erotic element in the sketch were her face and eyes, so fragile and frightened that they broke your heart. A wonderfully pathetic invitation.

It would be a big ring that Megan and I would choose.

I carefully put the picture in my bag. No way did I want to wake up in the middle of the night and see it.

I scribbled a note to her first thing in the morning and slipped it into her hand when the runners came in for their coffee.

Odessa my love,

Thank you for the sketch of the most beautiful woman in all the world. Now you know her as well as I do.

Love,

Ivan.

Tears in her wide brown eyes, she nodded at me.

It was the day of the Christmas Ball at the club. Usually our family pretty much ignored it. This year we were all going. To celebrate our grand duchess.

I own a tux which I do everything possible to avoid wearing. I might have to wear it a lot more in years to come.

In the afternoon I was dispatched to collect five special red and green Christmas ties and cummerbunds, the fifth for the kid from St. Ignatius chosen by Brigid.

I bounded back into the house, only to find it empty. Women kind must engage in many preparations for a night like this.

I bounded upstairs, hoping that Odessa was around so we could laugh at the absurd male decorations, as though we were members of a wedding party.

The door to her room was slightly ajar. I peeked in. The faithful wolfhound was sound asleep. Odessa was standing by the mirror, carefully brushing her luminous black hair. She was wearing the most minimal of undergarments, appropriate perhaps for a Brazilian beach and for the gown she would wear in a few hours.

"Ivan," she exclaimed, putting down the brush and retreating a few steps.

"You said it was all right to admire the human form," I reminded her.

"So long as one does it respectfully."

"Am I not admiring with respect?"

She gulped.

"Hungry respect," she said.

She lowered her eyes as a flush spread over her face and neck and chest.

"Come here," I said.

She did. Eyes still lowered, she stood close to me.

"Are you afraid of me, Tatiana Alekseevna?" I said, tilting her head up so I could see her eyes.

"A little bit," she said. "Not much. It is a kind of nice fear."

"Ivan the Nice."

She nodded.

"You know I won't hurt you?"

She nodded again.

"Or do anything bad to you?"

"Of course not. I trust Ivan the Wonderful."

Part of me wished I was not quite so wonderful.

I touched her belly lightly with my fingers and then the tops of her breasts. She sighed deeply.

I kissed her on the forehead and said, "See you later in this immoral dress of yours."

"Thank you, Ivan. I'm glad you like me."

"How could I not . . . and as for you, Good Doggie Fiona, a hell of a guard you are!"

"If it were not you," the grand duchess said, as she picked up her hairbrush, "she would have been instantly awake. She trusts you too."

A very big ring, I told myself as I staggered downstairs, still holding the ties and cummerbunds. June wedding. Definitely.

The dress, it turned out, was far from immoral. Dazzling, devastating, sensational perhaps, bound to attract attention, but quite moral.

We cheered for the grand duchess, now truly looking like one in a white evening gown with trim of Christmas red and green, when she walked down the stairs—Brigie had modified it so that it no longer looked like a teenage prom dress. Her braids were piled high on her head and held in place by a red ribbon which might just as well have been a diadem.

"That can't be my date," I protested. "A woman like that would never go to the Christmas Ball with a punk like Jackie Flanigan."

Much laughter. The family was still mellowed out.

"Do I look all right, Ivan?" she asked anxiously

in the car. "I do not want to embarrass you and your family."

"You won't embarrass us, Odessa. How do you feel?"

"I feel wonderful. I've never been to a Christmas ball before. I don't know how to act, but I know I will have a good time. You must help me, Ivan."

"That's why I'll be there, not that you'll need much of my help."

She glided into the lobby of the club like it was her own personal castle.

"Is that your trophy?" she pointed to a glass case. "Oh it must be! Your name is on it after all the others! See! John Mahoney Flanigan. And it doesn't say punk either."

"Yeah."

"This should be at your house?"

"Well . . ."

"You must ask one of the nice men if you can take it home with you. That way you will make peace during this season of peace."

"No."

"Yes."

"No."

"Yes."

"All right, yes!"

So we danced. We drank only small sips of white wine, so intoxicated were we with one another. I danced with the women in my family, she with the men, even Doctor. Maria said what everyone was thinking.

"People will say, Jack, that you're awfully lucky to have found such a woman. I think you're both terribly lucky. Take good care of her."

"I couldn't do anything else, Maria," I answered, "But there's nothing definite between us. We've only known each other for two months."

"Bring her back next Christmas; we all need our Russian Daystar."

"You dance very well, Ivan," Odessa said to me, when we were back in one another's arms. "You should go to more balls."

"Only with beautiful dates."

"Silly."

Later we were sitting at our table while the orchestra was taking a break.

"Tell us a story, Aunt Tati," Steph begged. "Another Christmas story for grown-ups ... or for those of us like Joe and me who want to be grown-ups."

My date nodded solemnly. "I will tell you the story of Babushka."

"Great," several of us said.

People from two of the neighboring tables turned around to listen. Then a hush settled on the whole noisy crowd, somehow drawn to the magic at our family table.

"Once upon a time, long, long ago, there lived a woman named Babushka. She had the cleanest, neatest house in the village and was the best cook in the village too. She painted the window frames white, picked the weeds out of her neat little garden every day, washed the walk in front of the house each morning when she woke up, swept the floors every day, washed them every week, painted the walls every six months. She said it was her job to teach by example the younger women in the village what a clean house should be like. Most of the women in the village, while they admired her house—who wouldn't—said that poor Babushka had nothing else to live for.

"Then one day there were rumors in the village of twelve kings—this is a Russian story and we believe that there were twelve kings because there are twelve apostles and twelve choirs of angels—who were crossing the desert to visit a newborn prince.

"Babushka paid no attention. She would not be distracted from the task of keeping a neat house. Besides she once had her own little prince and that was enough for her. The memories of the little prince, long since gone to God, still made tears come to her eyes.

"Well, a few days later there was tumult outside, horns and drums and sackbuts, bells and cymbals, the cries of men and horses and camels. All of it was just outside her house.

"She ran to the door and found twelve men in the most wonderful sable and crimson and purple robes and long trains and giant turbans waiting for her. They all bowed deeply when they saw Babushka.

" 'Madam,' said a dark man in white robes, with yet another deep bow, 'We are twelve kings who have come on a long journey across the desert searching for the little prince about whom we have learned from yonder bright star. We believe we have found his village. We humbly request food and lodging for the night so we can pay our respects to him on the morrow and bring him the treasures that are his due.'

" 'At my house!'

" 'We are told that you have the cleanest house in the village and are the best cook. If you do not wish us to stay with you . . .'

"Babushka believed in hospitality. So she invited them in and asked some of the young women of the village to help. She prepared a huge dinner for these hungry men who had traveled so far in search of the little prince—caviar, three kinds of potatoes, good strong Russian beef with wonderful sauce, and three different kinds of Russian ice cream.

"Of course she gave them each one glass good vodka, and no more than one.

"While they were eating and drinking, she scurried upstairs and made sure that all the beds in her six guest rooms were freshly made.

"I do not know why she had that many rooms, but the story says she did.

"Then she worked all night washing the dishes and cleaning the kitchen and the dining room and preparing breakfast. When the twelve kings came down in the morning, they found a wonderful Russian breakfast waiting for them— salmon and sausage and potatoes and eggs and a huge samovar of the best Russian tea.

"When they were finished, they thanked her

again, bowed solemnly, and took their leave. The dark man in the white gown tarried a moment.

" 'My lady Babushka,' he said. 'You have been most gracious. Why do you not accompany us to see the little prince?'

"Babushka thought that was a wonderful idea and promised to join them in the village as soon as she cleaned up her house. She set to work getting rid of the mess the twelve kings had left—kings are like most men, they make terrible messes. She scrubbed all the dishes and pots and pans and put them away; she stripped off the sheets, washed them, and remade the beds. She mopped the floor and the walk down to the street and pulled a few weeds out of the garden. She would have washed the walls too, but she was just too tired to do this."

Now thirty or forty people were gathered around our table listening to the story. The larger the audience, the better the storyteller became.

"Finally she went to the cupboard where she had kept for so many years the toys of her own little prince. Why keep them any longer? Why not give them to the living prince, instead of preserving them for the dead one? So she cleaned and dusted all the toys and packed them in a basket.

You can't give a prince toys with dust on them.

"Then she suddenly was so tired that she sat down, the basket in her lap, to relax for just a minute or two. Her weary eyes closed, just for a couple of seconds.

"She woke up suddenly. The sun was rising in the east. Had she slept all day and all night?

"Frantic now, she grabbed the basket and ran into the village. There were no camels, no horses, no tambourines, no chimes, no drums, no kings. The center of the village was as quiet as it used to be.

"She asked an old man sitting on a bench where the little prince and his mother were.

" 'They left yesterday,' he said, 'In the afternoon after the twelve kings visited them. It is said that wicked King Herod wants to kill the little prince. The mother and father and child are somewhere out in the desert.'

"Babushka immediately ran into the desert after them. They say that even today she is still searching. Whenever she hears of a newborn boy child—or in our time a newborn girl child also—she rushes to the child's side to see if it is the little prince. But she has not found him yet. However, she always leaves a toy for the child and rushes on. Her basket never empties. She knows that someday she will find the little prince and give him all the toys. But she has, as I say, never found him.

"I don't like the way the story ends. I think she found him in Egypt after a long search. However, the story of poor Babushka who confused the important with the essential should be a warning to us never to forget what Christmas means: Love has come into the world and is looking for our response."

The audience had been listening intently, alternatively amused and somber. Tears glistened in the eyes of many of the women, including of course all the Flanigan women. Grand applause. Many congratulations.

"Gave us a lot to think about," was the most frequent comment to the modest, blushing storyteller.

As well it might.

Our bright morning star had worked a few miracles. My contentious and difficulty family had been transformed. The metamorphosis would not last long. However, during the interlude of peace and good will some of them might find a window of opportunity, perhaps one with a candle in it, to alter slightly the direction of their lives. Maria might hate a little less. Steph might realize how fortunate she was to have found Joe. Maybe Eddie would leave Brigid alone. Possibly I could give up most of my grudges.

That's how grace works, I guess.

Then I was pressed to sing a few Christmas songs. I was not going to become an Irish whisky tenor. However, in Odessa's presence and having promised to make peace with the club, what choice did I have? I led them in "O Holy Night," "The First Noel," and "We Three Kings." I introduced the last one with apologies to any Orthodox who might be present and believed there were twelve.

Then I decided, what the hell!

"You may have noticed that my date tonight is a striking young woman who shows no taste in whom she accepts as an escort. She is Russian actually. Her name is Tatiana. There is a lovely aria in the opera *Eugene Onegin*, second act, about a woman named Tatiana. She has been kind of a daystar for our family this Christmas. I'm sure you won't mind if I sing the aria in her honor."

Of course they wouldn't mind.

The subject of the celebration blushed and lowered her eyes. But she didn't fight it either.

> *"Come let us celebrate, congratulate*
> *Our lovely lady on this day*
> *Her sweet and charming ways*
> *Bring joy to all our days*
> *And so may it always be*
> *Long may you shine, beautiful Tatiana!*
> *Long may you shine, beautiful Tatiana!*

> *"May fortune always give joy*
> *to each day she lives*
> *On her may life ever smile*
> *Let her life be like a star*
> *Shining always from afar*
> *Lighting our night and day!*
> *Long may you shine, beautiful Tatiana!*
> *Long may you shine, beautiful Tatiana!"*

I sang it a second time as I had at her apartment. The crowd joined in the refrains. They cheered until Odessa stood up and bowed.

We took the golf trophy home too.

CHAPTER

6

Finally it was time to fly back to Harvard. Odessa and I were both exhausted and happy to leave. My family continued to be unbearably mellow. We were both hugged often before we left.

Mom took me aside at the last minute.

"She is a wonderful young woman, Jack. I'm sure you know that."

"I do."

"She is an angel. She gave us the happiest Christmas we have ever enjoyed."

"I noticed."

"You must bring her here every Christmas. She has not cured anything, but she has given us a chance to grow a little."

"That's all grace can do."

"Yes, I know. We want her here every Christmas."

"That could be difficult," I said realizing that there would be more to the task than going ring-shopping with the good Meg.

"She's obviously in love with you."

"Is she? I'm not so sure."

"We want her back, Jack. Do you understand?"

"I'll see what I can do."

If I did persuade her to take the ring Meg and I would choose, I would have a grand time telling the family.

No, she would have to tell them.

That's called counting your chickens before they're hatched.

When we piled out of the cab at O'Hare—it was snowing of course—and turned our luggage in, I told her the family's sentiment.

"They want you back, Odessa. Every year. You made Christmas for them. I have been ordered to bring you back."

She jumped in dismay.

"Ivan, that cannot be! These days were wonderful, but I have so many things to do with my life. . . . I can make no promises to anyone. It is quite impossible."

I'd misread the signs. How could I have missed them so completely? Flanigan, you blew it again.

"It's your call, of course."

"Thank you."

I wished that the earth would open up and swallow me. How could I have been so wrong? There would be no happy chat with Megan the next morning.

We waited silently for the call to board our plane. An hour late. What do you expect at O'Hare during the holidays?

Mentally I kicked myself repeatedly for my stupidity. How insensitive can one dumb South Side Irishman be?

Then I argued to myself that I was in fact relieved. I was too young to marry anyway. Why give up my bachelor freedom? No way. Not for many years.

In truth I was so sad that I felt for the first time in my life that my heart might break.

I had been unable to upgrade. We were stuck half way down the aisle in the coach class of one of those horrible MD-80s. I gave her the window and took the middle seat for myself.

She held my hand as we took off.

Then she curled up in her seat, leaned on my

shoulder, and prepared to go to sleep.

"Ivan?"

"Yes?"

"I said 'quite impossible,' did I not?"

"You did."

"That does not mean absolutely impossible."

"It doesn't?"

"Not at all."

"I'm glad to hear it."

She snuggled closer to me.

"Good."

Then she added sleepily, "Even nightingales can't live on fairy tales."

Was she the nightingale and I the real world? Who cares!

She slept all the way to Logan.

I was too happy to sleep.

With the grace of God and a little bit of luck and care with my loud mouth, I would have my own personal bright daystar for the rest of my life.

I hummed love songs softly to myself.

Irish love songs.

Russian love songs too.

Soon we'd be singing them together.

Turn the page for a preview of

A Christmas Wedding

by Andrew M. Greeley

Now available from Tom Doherty Associates

No one offered to help Rosemarie clean up. As usual, I stayed after the others to help remove the glasses and the empty bags of potato chips, and to vacuum the carpet. Her apartment was small and frequently chaotic, but it was expensively furnished and carpeted. I knew that if I didn't designate myself as the clean-up brigade, Rosemarie would let the job go till the morning and possibly the morning after that.

"Chucky," she would say to me, "unlike you, I can sleep at night if the apartment is a mess. I'll clean it up eventually."

"I learned my housekeeping habits from the good April."

We would both laugh because my mother was, to put it mildly, relaxed in her approach to housekeeping.

We were perhaps potential lovers, though both of us would vigorously deny it. We were friends, a much more relaxed and, I told myself, safer alliance. Rosemarie dated others, often Ed Murray, my old-time football rival from Mount Carmel, and I of course dated no one.

Sometimes Rosemarie dragged me back to her apartment for hamburgers or sandwiches and an occasional fruit salad. "You'll die if you eat that University food or Jimmy's hamburgers all the time."

"It's no worse than what they fed us at the Dome."

"And look what happen to you there, storing beer under the bed, of all things."

I had been thrown out on that charge, though I didn't drink beer or anything else, and had been framed.

Sometimes we were very serious, even personal. She more than I.

"Daddy put all that property and money in Mommy's name so that if he was ever in trouble at the Exchange they wouldn't be able to take it away from him."

"Unable to meet his margin calls."

"Whatever. Anyway, she hated him so much before she died that she made a will and left it all to me in such a way that he couldn't touch any of the property. Or the bank accounts. He's furious. Mr. O'Laughlin, Daddy's lawyer, is after me all the time about it."

Since shortly before the Flood, I think, Joe O'Laughlin had enjoyed the reputation of being the most dishonest lawyer on the West Side, a perfect legal adviser for Jim Clancy.

"Will you sign it all over to him, then?" We were talking in whispers since we were in a library reading room. I couldn't remember how we had entered this strange conversation.

"I'm not sure. What do you think I ought to do? Mommy wanted me to have it all."

"Was it hers to give? I mean, he really owned all those buildings, didn't he? It was just a legal fiction."

"Was it, Chuck?" she tapped a pencil against her lips. "Dad used her money to begin his investments at the Exchange after his mother died. She said that was the only reason he married her."

Small wonder that the young woman was a little crazy.

"Do you hate your father?"

She stared up at the ceiling of Harper Library. "He's so lonely and unhappy."

"You don't live at home because of the fight over your mother's will?"

"It's not a fight exactly. I mean, we're not enemies because of it. I think he did love her and didn't know how to express it. Wouldn't that be terrible?"

I agreed that it would. And hoped that she would change the subject. I did, however, manage to touch her hand sympathetically.

"Stop distracting me," she said, grinning, "and get back to your Pascal."

I hated Jim Clancy. When I was a kid, he took me out in a sailboat on Lake Geneva and deliberately got me seasick. Then, after I had vomited over the side of the boat at the Clancy pier, he shoved a chocolate ice-cream bar at my face. I vomited again, unfortunately missing him.

"He has always liked his little practical jokes," my mom sighed, "poor man. First one, then, your guard is down, another."

"Once, at Twin Lakes," my father added, "he set off the fire alarm. Then when the firemen had gone back to Walworth, he threw stink bombs into two of the washrooms and started real fires."

"Very funny," I commented.

I had hated him because he was rich. Now I had another reason to hate him.

I returned to the agonized, contorted, ecstatic reflections of that great, God-haunted man. Out of the corner of my eye I noted that Rosemarie was still staring at the ceiling. Still wrestling with a puzzle, I thought.

And I don't want to know what it is.

I was troubled by the mystery surrounding her mother's death when I was away in the Army, in Europe. My parents and sisters, normally immune to secrecy, refused to discuss the matter when I asked direct questions, and they avoided any hints when I tried to approach it indirectly.

"Mrs. Clancy's death must have been a terrible shock to Rosemarie?"

"Rosie is a pretty tough young woman," my dad would answer, not even looking up from his copy of the Chicago *Sun*.

There had been, I learned from press clippings, a police investigation and a coroner's report that Mrs. Clancy had died an "accidental" death from an unfortunate fall down the stairs into the basement of the Clancy home at 1105 North Menard.

Pushed down the stairs? By her husband? By Rosemarie? Drunk?

It was none of my business. Yet I remembered hearing her sob in St. Ursula's late one night. Life in that family would drive anyone to drink.

Whatever had happened, she was still admired—no, adored—in the O'Malley family. Yet despite my mother's blunt if clichéd comment about felines and curiosity, I wanted more details. I never asked Rosemarie about the accident. That would have been gratuitously cruel.

We joked that we would be incompatible marriage partners. Rosemarie was a morning person. She bounded out of bed with full-steam energy. The eight-thirty class was her favorite of the day. I on the other hand did not join the human race (her words) till ten-fifteen.

I flourished at midday, when Rosemarie began to think of a nap. And I crashed early in the evening, when she had acquired her second wind.

"It wouldn't work, Chuck. Our schedules would be so different that we'd never produce children."

"You're absolutely right."

But even in my groggy, early-morning daze, she still seemed gorgeous, a potential bed partner who would be attractive at all hours of the day.

And if Mom's snapshots of Rosemarie's grandmother were any basis for judgment, at all the times of her life.

"Rosie has such fine facial bones, Chucky dear, and a naturally splendid figure. If she takes care of herself, she'll be lovely all her life."

"Did her grandmother drink too much?"

"Not at all," Mom replied, ignoring the implication of my question, as she frequently did. "Neither did her mother until after she married."

Then the good April added one of her non sequitur comments that only seemed irrelevant. "Most women would die to have a waist that slim."

"Skinny, emaciated," I replied.

Mom and Dad both chuckled. I had indeed protested too much and thus admitted my interest in Rosemarie's body. I'd have to be more careful.

"Well, the poor little thing could use five or six more pounds."

"More like ten."

"And maybe that would slow her down on the tennis court, huh, Chucky?" my father asked, with no respect for his son's mediocre athletic ability.

"Well," I said, deliberately trying to shock, "she sure has great teats!"

The good April, whom I had expected to reprove me for my language, only sighed and said, "I'm surprised you noticed, dear."

Would Rosemarie be as attractive in her middle forties as the good April? And as sexually appealing as the good April was to my father?

Such questions, I warned myself sternly, were not appropriate. You'll mess up something good if you even think about them. Naturally, I thought about them all the time. In Bamberg I'd had a lover, a young woman I had planned to bring home as my wife. She disappeared after I had saved her and her mother and sister from the Ruskies, who would have raped them to death. I had never found her. I had learned from her, however, the pleasures of sexual love. A least I thought it was love. It was certainly pleasurable. Trudi had been a straightforward young woman, fighting to stay alive. Our affair, if it could be called that, was straightforward, uncomplicated. Rosemarie was much more problematic.

What would happen if they ever met? Thank God there wasn't much chance of that ever happening.

Rosemarie was a good friend, loyal and helpful. I enjoyed being with her and she seemed to enjoy mothering me. We were not suited to be lovers, I insisted mentally, but we might well be lifelong friends.

We even went to an occasional film in the early evening, and during the seasons to the opera and the symphony. We did not hold hands. People do that on dates, you see, but we were two friends watching a movie or an opera together, not a couple on a date.

Was I kidding myself? Of course.

Did I realize I was kidding myself?

To tell the truth, I can't remember. Not that it mattered.

We saw Eliot's *Murder in the Cathedral* and agreed that the last temptation was indeed the greatest treason, to do the right thing for the wrong reason.

Neither of us thought that we might ever do that in our lives.

And we saw Christopher Fry's *The Lady's Not for Burning* and argued about whether Rosemarie was like the heroine, I taking the affirmative position and she the negative.

"I'm not that smart."

"You are too."

"Or that good."

"Better."

(Storm clouds gathering). "Don't say dumb things, Chucky, when you don't know what you're talking about."

We listened in awe to Fry's *A Sleep of Prisoners* on tape and agreed that we thanked God that our time was now, when the enterprise was exploration into God.

We didn't know what that meant.

There were no romantic exchanges between me and Rosemarie at that point. In fact, we avoided touching as though it would transmit an infectious disease. Both of us were satisfied with our friendship and did not want to risk endangering it with romance.

At least that's how I reasoned, though it's clear from the way I write about her today that she had become an obsession, a delightful and mysterious obsession. I had no idea how Rosemarie viewed the matter. Could not a man and a woman spend a couple of hours every day with each other, take care of each other, listen to each other's hopes and ideas, and occasionally sit next to each other in a theater without having to worry about love or sex?

The answer obviously is no. Not at our stage in life anyway. And not with a woman as spectacularly attractive as Rosemarie.

"Do you go to bed with her?" one of my classmates asked as we left the library and Rosemarie slipped away in the direction of her next class.

"Oh, no, we're just friends. We were practically raised together."

"I'd say she was a distracting friend."

"After awhile you hardly notice."

Lie.

"Thank you for the help," she said when we had put away the last glass on the night of the session with Père Danielou. "You make a great kitchen maid."

"Faithful servant."

She hesitated, made a face, and then said, "Chucky, you shouldn't look at me that way during talks."

"What way?" I asked, feigning innocence.

"Ogling me, like you did during poor Père Danielou's talk."

When an Irishwoman uses the adjective "poor," it invariably serves as a warning that the person in question is temporarily immune from criticism.

"You don't like it when a man ogles you?"

"It depends on the man." A rose tint appeared on her face.

"Ah?"

"I don't mind it from you because you look at me so sweetly, but you shouldn't do it during a lecture."

"People notice?"

"Certainly not! I notice! You should pay attention to great men like Père Danielou."

For my own good.

Did she know what was the content of my sweet reveries? I almost asked her, and then realized that the ice beneath me was getting very thin. "As your faithful servant, I hear and obey."

"A little mouthy, but basically all right . . . Charles C. O'Malley, look at that snow! Eight inches already. I'm not going to let you drive home in that funny little car. You can stay in my guest room."

Gulp.

"It's not that bad."

"It is too." She reached for the phone. "I absolutely forbid you to go out in it."

"But I have to—"

She waved me to silence. "April? Rosemarie. Sorry to call so late but I am not going to let your older son drive all the way back to the West Side in this weather. . . . I'm glad you agree. You know how much he likes to play the hero. . . . Oh, I'll lock him in the guest room. And, anyway, you know how he is. He doesn't go in for that sort of thing."

Triumphantly she handed the phone to me.

"Rosemarie is perfectly right, dear," Mom said, trying to sound severe. "You can't drive home tonight. You stay there till the streets are cleaned."

"Yes, ma'am."

"And be good."

"Mom! You know me. I wouldn't even think of not being good."

"That's what I'm afraid of, dear."

Rosemarie promptly ushered me to the guest room, pointed to the bathroom, and waved good night. I inspected the room. Very neat. Nothing out of place. I took off my khaki sweatshirt and hung it up neatly. I folded my fatigue trousers so that the creases were perfectly in line and hung them up too. Then, in my old but serviceable GI shorts, I knelt down for my nightly prayers, a custom I had begun in Germany when there was no one else in the room and then resumed after my expulsion from Notre Dame to reassure the Deity that my problem was not with Him, but with the Catholic Church and especially the Congregation of the Holy Cross.

I am sorry, I informed Him, if I took excessive delight in imagining Rosemarie without her clothes. I tried to be respectful. She even thinks that I ogle her sweetly. I wonder what she means by that and what she thinks I'm doing. However, I hold You partially to blame because You made her so attractive and me so horny. You know that I would never do anything to hurt her. I am in somewhat unusual circumstances tonight, compromising, one might say. Like a lot of bad movie plots. If You ask me, and You rarely do, I think the good April went along a little too easily with this situation. Besides, I'm too tired tonight for romance. If it is all the same with You, however, I'd just as soon fall asleep instantly so my imagination won't run wild. I could do without the dreams too.

God apparently heard my final prayer. Clad in my shorts, and having dispossessed one of Rosemarie's teddy bears, I fell asleep as soon as my head hit the pillow. If she did indeed lock the door, I thought in the last few seconds of consciousness, she did it very quietly.

"Are you awake and decent?" I heard her voice from a great distance.

"Yes to the latter"—I rolled over and buried my head in the pillow—"and no to the former."

She propelled herself through the door, a tray laden with bacon, eggs, toast, raspberry jam, and tea in her hands, a newspaper under her arm.

"My hotel provides these services erratically," she announced briskly. "Guests are advised to take advantage of them while they can."

She put the tray on the bed next to me, bustled over to the window, and pulled open the drapes, illuminating the little bedroom with glittering winter sunlight reflected in a thousand icicles, a ballroom in a fairy wonderland.

Rosemarie was a tidal wave of fresh energy, a robust, well-scrubbed erotic presence, a clean and healthy promise of coming springtime. You realized that she was also a well calculated and discreet temptation only when you had been lured into her glowingly wholesome trap.

In other words, that morning she had designed herself to be an interesting hint of what it might be like to wake up next to her every morning.

Much too energetic for my tastes, but it might be pleasurable to be swept up in that energy.

She was wearing a tightly belted white satin robe. Her freshly brushed hair hung neatly to her shoulders, her face glowed from a recent shower, and she smelled of soap and inviting scent.

A carefully arranged entry.

"The maid service in this hotel," I observed, rubbing my eyes, "is loud, pushy, and extremely attractive."

"Thank you, sir." She bowed. "And a good morning to you too."

"The door wasn't locked?"

"Really, Chucky"—she waved her hand—"I have a lot of more serious worries than defending myself from your amorous intentions."

"You don't think you could seduce me?"

"I didn't say that and you know it. I said I wasn't afraid of your seducing me."

"Ah."

I would doubtless make a mess of it.

"Chuck," John Raven had told me, "your tragic flaw with women is that you help them when they're vulnerable. So naturally they fall in love with you. You can't resist a vulnerable woman who is in love with you."

"I've resisted a couple of them."

"Just barely."

Rosemarie waved her hand again. "Not that it wouldn't be interesting to see you try."

"High comedy."

The wave was becoming a familiar gesture. It was a little flick, upward and outward, of her right hand. It said that I was perhaps an amusing little boy, but wasn't it time, after all, that I began to grow up? However, the implication was always of patient, maternal affection.

The wave almost always melted my heart. It offered me warmth and comfort and a secure spot on the desert island she brought with her. Secure, but not necessarily restful.

"Anyway"—she sat on the edge of my bed—"your wife, whoever she's going to be, poor woman, will have to resign herself to love between eleven and noon, because that is the only time you'll be wide enough awake to have sex on your mind."

Her robe slipped away, to reveal a touch of ivory thigh.

"I suppose you're right." I sighed. "I mean you can't make love with raspberry jam on your fingers."

"*You* couldn't anyway. . . . So what do you think?"

"About love with raspberry jam?"

"About last night, silly. And the whole business."

"I'm a lot happier here than I was at Notre Dame," I began.

She nodded. "That's obvious."

"I've studied harder than I thought I possibly could. My head reels sometimes from all the ideas. I've learned more about Catholicism from your friends than I did in sixteen years of Catholic schools. It's exciting. What more can I say?"

"Better than Notre Dame in everyway?"

"No." I thought about the rest of my answer. "You and I share some basic values with the guys at

Notre Dame that we don't with many of the people here. Notre Dame is less arrogant, and heaven knows it has reason to be less arrogant than this place; and loyalty—what we'd think of as loyalty anyway—is almost invisible here. But universities are about ideas and there are a lot more ideas in a day here than in a semester at Notre Dame."

"The people last night?" she drew the robe over her thigh.

"They're not St. Ursula people, Rosemarie. Not that everyone has to be. But they're something new in the Church and I think there will be a lot more of them."

"And what they stand for will eventually affect St. Ursula's and everything else in the Church. Our children"—she blushed deeply and tightened the belt on her robe but did not completely cover her delicious thigh—"in separate families, will live differently because of their ideas."

"Maybe," I admitted.

Which turned out to be an understatement. But then no one, not even someone as perspicacious as Rosemarie, could have anticipated the Vatican Council.

"And you?" she persisted.

"Early morning catechism?"

"Why else did you think I kept you here all night?" Her grim lips indicated that she was not joking. "I wanted to catch you off guard."

"With me in my GI shorts and you in that lovely robe?"

"Shut up"—she poked at my naked ribs with a quick, sharp finger—"and answer my question."

"Yes, Mommy." I ducked away from her tickling jab.

"Well, someone like you needs at least two mommies."

"I ask myself sometimes what a would-be accountant and an occasional photographer—"

"Too occasional, but go on."

"—needs with so much heavy thought and so many tantalizing ideas."

She rose from the bed and walked over to the sun-filled window. I squinted to watch the satin-covered back. Yes indeed, a perfectly acceptable rear end too. Maybe I would shock the good April with that comment. ("I've just noticed, April Mae, that Rosemarie has a lovely ass.")

"Accountants are members of the human race too, Chuck. They need ideas and vision as much as anyone else. Besides, you're a lot more than just a potential accountant with a camera."

"What am I then?"

She turned to face me, a living statue bathed in wonderful backlight that turned her long dark hair to black fire. "I'm not sure," she said slowly and carefully, choosing every word, "but I know you're someone with the mark of greatness."

"Come on, Rosemarie, that's a romantic day-dream."

"No it isn't. But hurry up and get dressed or you'll miss your first class."

She spun toward me again at the door of the room.

"You really ought to give yourself more time."

Front-lighted now, she was a creature of pure, radiant light, not a faerie sprite over a bog but a seraph from next to the throne of God. I would have to bring along my camera the Kodak C-3 she had given me, and not the Leica that had been Trudi's gift, and open once again my Rosemarie archive.

"More time?"

"To think, to reflect, to pray, to play. You have to stop filling every second of your day with obligations."

At that moment I could have lost myself forever in the luminosity of the goddess looking down on me.

"You don't need a degree and a job, Rosemarie. I do. I admire the way you study. I wish I could concentrate on learning too. But . . ."

"Why can't you?"

I didn't have a quick answer.

"See!" she proclaimed triumphantly, turned again, and departed from the room in a rustle of satin and a cloud of light.

So our early morning tête-à-tête was finished. Rosemarie had said what she wanted to say. And chosen the circumstances, complete with the halo of backlight, to say it forcefully.

She would be a superb lover, I told myself, if she were not crazy. Last night she was wonderful. The night before she was so drunk she could have been raped behind the bar or have frozen to death on the way home. Do you want to spend the rest of your life with someone like that?

The answer was obvious.

And the proper conclusion was that, regardless of her radiance that morning as a creature of pure light, she was a threat. The friendship could not go on forever.

Somehow I would have to end our romance after the spring quarter.

Still, when I returned that evening to Oak Park, I informed the good April, when she had asked how the night at Rosie's had been, that I had discovered she had a quite adequate rear end.

I expected a reaction of shock at my observation. Instead she replied, "Well, dear, I'm surprised you noticed that too. You're making good progress."

In my prayers that night, I asked God, Was that an offer, do You think? Was Rosemarie offering to be my wife, in the long term of course? What do You mean, I should know the answer to that? Have You forgotten what she was like the night before? You think that if I'm not willing to take the risk with her, I should get out of the relationship while I can?

Or is it too late already?

What do You mean, that's not the question?

You're telling me the question is whether I want to get out, whether I've ever wanted to get out?

That's not a fair question.

Anyway, what can she possibly see in me?

No answer to that question?